Praise for Gia Dawn's *Dunmore Rising*

Nymph Rating: 4.5 Nymphs "Gia Dawn has written a story with positive role models for women and the men who love and respect them. The love that Jiliana and Graham have for each other is what keeps them together through the rough times. I can't say enough praises about this series that Gia has written."

~ *Goddess Minx, Literary Nymphs Reviewer*

"Full of passion and peril, DUNMORE RISING, the fourth book in the Demons of Dunmore series, stands well on its own, even as it gives readers a glimpse into the lives of previous heroes and heroines. If you're looking for an emotional, passionate story with a touch of magic, look no further."

~ *Lori Ann, Romance Reviews Today*

Look for these titles by
Gia Dawn

Now Available:

Demons of Dunmore
Lord Demon's Delight (Book 1)
Lady Strumpet (Book 2)
Princess of Thieves (Book 3)

Love and Lore: A Fairy Special Gift

Print Anthology
Love and Lore

Dunmore Rising

Demons of Dunmore

Gia Dawn

A SAMHAIN PUBLISHING, LTD. publication.

Samhain Publishing, Ltd.
577 Mulberry Street, Suite 1520
Macon, GA 31201
www.samhainpublishing.com

Dunmore Rising
Copyright © 2009 by Gia Dawn
Print ISBN: 978-1-60504-163-6
Digital ISBN: 978-1-60504-052-3

Editing by Angela James
Cover by Anne Cain

First Samhain Publishing, Ltd. electronic publication: June 2008
First Samhain Publishing, Ltd. print publication: April 2009

Dedication

For my great friends Mike and Glen. And Sufu Tim, Sufu Mike and Sufu Dickie, master teachers extraordinaire.

Prologue

Snapdragon, Pansy, and Rose fluttered nervously outside Graham Dunmore's bedchamber door, casting suspicious glances at the giggling women lounging on his bed.

"Does he really plan to top them all?" Rose snapped her fingers and a fan appeared in front of her face. She sighed when the cool breeze hit her heated cheeks.

"Says he plans on breaking a family record." Snapdragon grinned wickedly. "And given the size of that great horn between his legs, he should succeed admirably."

Pansy glowered. "Shouldn't we stop him or something? It doesn't seem right—"

"What?" Snapdragon interrupted. "That he should have a bit of fun? We've worked him to the bone lately...no pun intended," she added with a chuckle.

Rose snickered behind her fan. "But hasn't he turned out well? The first Dunmore ever knighted."

All three fairies looked with pride at the newly slimmed giant who strode completely naked into the room, sending his five paid companions into another fit of giggles. Not an ounce of fat marred the sleekly muscled body dripping with water from his recent bath. He'd cut his hair short and the blond locks stood up in wet spikes, framing the hollows of his cheeks and the hard line of his jaw.

"He is a fine looking man," Rose whispered in admiration, her cheeks pinking again.

The object of their adoration turned and gave them a loathing look. "Get the hell away from me," he snapped, moving to slam the door in their faces.

"Well, of all the ungrateful—" Pansy's expression darkened and she lifted a hand high in the air. Snapdragon smacked it down and the two fairies glared at each other in open animosity.

Rose took the arm of each and floated them into another room. "Let him have this one last fling," she said, pouring them all a glass of ale. "This is the very last time he'll ever get a chance to break that family record."

"Then we should wish him the best of luck!" Their laughter rippled through the air as they raised their glasses in a toast.

Chapter One

Graham glared across the table at both his mothers. "I do not have to do everything the two—no, five—of you say." He glowered at the three tiny fairy-godmothers calmly sitting at a table floating on the air.

To his continued horror, the women and fairies had formed an alliance that not even the king's army had any chance of breaking. He looked for support from his eldest brother, Llewellyn, who suddenly became overly busy with the baby cooing in his arms.

Graham let his expression remain cold as he stood and threw down a half-eaten piece of bread. "Whatever idiot scheme you have thought up now, I refuse to be a part of. Do you hear me?"

Finella's eyes narrowed, causing Graham to take a slight step back. "At least talk to the girl. Who knows, you might still like her."

Again Graham appealed to Llew. "Like her? Brother, will you kindly tell these...*ladies*...that liking doesn't have a damn thing to do with it. No knight has a woman for a squire. Ever!"

Llew ducked his head even further, as if that were at all possible. "Uh...ah..." He cleared his throat several times.

"Bastard," Graham muttered, running a hand through his hair. Had they all gone completely crazy?

First, his mothers had taken to the miserable fairies like they had been friends all their lives, settling Snapdragon, Pansy and Rose into their estate with a speed even the great plague couldn't match.

Then, they had agreed with Queen Amanda that Graham would be honored to watch over the prince regent as he competed in his first summer tournament—all without the man's knowledge, of course. And now, they had gone and hired a woman—WOMAN—to be his squire.

He couldn't decide if they were trying to get him killed, or laughed out of Westmyre.

Samantha smiled and motioned to one of the fairies to fly over and pour him another glass of wine. Graham knew it was Rose by the bright pink color of her gown.

"'Tis not like we hired just any girl," Samantha soothed. "This is Jiliana. You know her. The two of you were very good friends when you were younger."

"All you have to do is give her a chance," Finella added. "She's just gotten back from her stay in Eastshyre. She's trained for years with their women warriors. They have a reputation for being as good as any man."

Graham snorted, unappeased in the least little bit. "Mother, I know you like to think that a woman is as good as any man, and while I agree with you most of the time," he hastened to say when her look darkened and the blue-gowned fairy raised a hand into the air, "this is not one of them. If you want me to watch over the blasted princeling, then I get to choose my own squire. End of story."

"Ah, Jiliana," Samantha gushed as the door opened behind him. "How nice of you to come. We were just telling Graham all about your training, weren't we son?"

"So I heard," came a wry familiar voice. "I also heard he

wasn't overly enamored of the idea." Out of the corner of his eye, Graham saw the woman circle around him. "'Tis good to see you haven't changed much. Still as big a grouch as you ever were."

He turned, his tongue forming another slew of words, and nearly bit it off when he saw his childhood buddy for the first time in over seven years. Surprised didn't begin to describe the stupid look he knew he had plastered on his face.

Gone was the plump-bodied girl of the past who followed him awkwardly around and mimicked every move he made. The woman who stood before him now was tall, broad-shouldered and supple as a finely made bow, curved and polished to a pristine sheen...and just as deadly, he thought in amazement.

She wore wide-legged breeches tied in a thick sash at her waist paired with a high-collared top that was cut short to show a peek of skin beneath. One hand rested on the hilt of a wickedly curved sword hanging by her hip, and her dark hair fell straight down her back with a fringe of bangs framing huge grey eyes. An amazing mouth was twisted into a softly mocking smirk, and when he lowered his gaze, her ripe round breasts seemed to swell before his eyes.

"What's the matter, Graham, forget how to talk?"

Furious that she'd caught him gawking, he folded his arms across his chest and stared her down. "'Tis Sir Graham, to you." Beautiful she might be, but this would not be a relationship of equals, and the sooner she knew it the better.

When her eyes widened he hoped she would challenge him. If she did, he would be within his rights to refuse her the position, no matter what his mothers might say. At last she nodded and gave him a slight bow. "Sir Graham," she corrected, a new respect coloring her voice.

"Hmph." He'd not expected her to be trained so well in the

etiquette of combat. It was to her credit that she was. "You understand what your duties will entail? You will help me in and out of my armor, polish it, wash my clothes—and me if necessary—bring food and drink when I need it...and anything else I can possibly think of."

Her nod was even less enthusiastic than before.

Good, Graham thought with a smirk. Making progress. By the time he was finished with her, she'd beg him not to hire her. "Come." Graham left the room without turning to see if she followed. He was ready to put the woman in her place. "Let's see what you can do."

Jiliana swallowed down her nervousness as she stared at the man in front of her. If she'd expected any glimmer of the boy she'd known in the past, she'd been sorely disappointed. Graham Dunmore had become a stern-faced giant she didn't know at all. Muscles rippled beneath his shirt, and his breeches hugged legs as strong and thick as tree trunks. She'd heard he spent hours drinking and lazing around the countryside, but that had obviously changed. For whatever reason, he'd shaped up and turned his life around, now moving with the grace and confidence of a warrior unmatched in size or skill.

He led her to the guards' chambers, a place she remembered well from her youth, ordering the men to bring him a sword and make ready the sparring grounds.

She shivered. Did he really intend to challenge her? Jiliana eyed him once more, searching for any sign of weakness. She couldn't find a thing. He was tall, but muscled enough to stay firmly rooted to the ground. She'd hoped his size had slowed down his speed, but when he was handed his sword and he spun to face her, she knew with a sinking heart he was as fast as he was strong...the perfect balance between earth and wind.

Before she could complete the thought, he swung the sword in an arc at her head. But she could see the blow was controlled, meant more to scare than to actually damage.

Jiliana rolled beneath the blade, springing up behind him, her own sword already in hand as he whirled and aimed a blow to her side. This time she parried, the force of his strike enough to numb her arm.

If this was Graham in control, the man would be deadly in an all out war.

Gritting her teeth against the throb that tingled from her fingers, she let his blade slide across her own, stepping to the side to land a solid boot to his thigh.

He whirled and she missed, barely catching herself as she stumbled backward, his elbow hitting her hard in the stomach. Sidestepping to soften the impact, she kicked high, slamming her foot into his shoulder.

He grunted, a wicked grin tilting up one corner of his lips. "Not bad," he grudgingly admitted, backhanding her in the chest. Although it took her breath away, Jiliana yielded to the blow, letting it knock her over, trying to use his force against him.

It was a move he hadn't expected. As she fell to the ground in a practiced drop, Graham lost his balance and tilted forward. Before he regained control, she scissored her legs around his calf, pulling his leg out from under him, rolling out of the way as he crashed beside her. She blinked back her surprise when one arm hooked around her waist and pulled her beneath him as he caught his weight on his other arm and his knees.

"I am impressed, Jili," he said, his eyes smiling down into hers. "I doubt any other man here could take you."

To her discomfort he made no move to pull away, regarding her with an intensity that stole her breath worse than the strike he'd delivered before. He traced a thumb over the scar that marred her jaw, the gesture tender and familiar.

Jiliana turned her face away, suddenly remembering this man knew everything about her. Secrets she'd refused to share with anyone else over the years; shame she'd refused to let anyone know for fear of the pity she'd see in their eyes. She would have to be careful not to repeat that mistake in the future. There were things in her life better left undiscovered.

His look continued to gentle, sympathy replacing his earlier abruptness. Disgusted with herself for not thinking through all the implications sooner, Jiliana shook her head and tried to push him off.

"You were right," she said in as calm a voice as she could manage, "this is not a good idea. But please tell your mothers how much I appreciated the offer."

His face softened even more, the expression intimate. It reminded her too much of their confidences in the past...confidences she now regretted with a passion even as she found herself wanting to confide in him once more.

"Where will you go?" He cupped her chin in his hand and forced her to face him. "Despite my earlier doubts, I was planning on offering you the position."

Eyes the color of a summer sky captured her gaze, refusing to let her look away. How could she not have seen just how handsome a man he truly was? High cheekbones angled over a strong jaw and full sensuous lips...lips made for—

With an effort, Jiliana pushed hard against his chest. This man was stirring in her all manner of needful things she'd sworn never to contemplate. A wretched pain clawed its way into her stomach. There were so many things she could not change.

Graham seemed to know every turn of her thoughts. "You

can trust me, Jili, same as you always have. I promise you that, and I am still a man of my word." In a fluid move he jumped to his feet, holding out a hand to help her from the ground. In the background she could hear the sound of men clapping. They had obviously enjoyed the show. Graham's smile grew wry. "I think they liked seeing me *almost* get my ass kicked."

Jiliana noticed he put the emphasis on almost. "Give me time to learn your weaknesses and I'll be able to take you down." She picked up her sword and glanced up at him through her lashes. Did he have any weaknesses? If he did, she couldn't find one...yet.

"Let me see your weapon," Graham ordered.

She handed him the blade, held out across both palms. "*Katana.*"

"Beautiful," he answered, looking at her, not the sword, as he plucked the *katana* from her hands.

Jiliana refused to flush. "'Tis a two body blade." When he raised a brow, she continued. "It can cut through two bodies with one stroke. There are legendary blades rated as five bodies or more...but it takes a much stronger arm than mine to use them to their full potential."

Graham would make perfect use of a blade that sharp and deadly. The thought sent a thrill racing up her spine. In his hands a master blade would find its ideal home.

"And the curve?" He ran his hand along the length of metal, a lover's touch, as he admired the craftsmanship.

"The curve doesn't form until the blade is quenched. The smith never knows if has done his job correctly until after the sword is removed from the water."

"I have never seen its equal." His expression was intimate as he handed her back her weapon.

Jiliana sheathed it easily. "'Twas given to me for saving the honor of a princess." Her thoughts turned bleak and her voice was bitter. "*Honor.* Another's honor I could save...but not my own."

She had sworn not to bring the subject up—no use crying over things you cannot change, the masters taught—but here she was, holding her failures out for him to see as she had done so often before. The weakness made her even more ashamed.

"Jili." Graham stepped close and ran his thumb over the scar on her jaw once more. "You were a child. Nothing was your fault. You cannot blame yourself for what they did to you."

She wanted to push his hand away and tell him what he could do with his pity, but in all the world, he was the only person she'd ever confided in, the only one who knew how much that terrible night had cost her...and how it had led to things he couldn't begin to imagine.

Before she could think of a single word in protest, he wrapped his great arms around her and pulled her close to his chest, resting his chin on her head. She blinked hard against her tears as the years slipped away and she was a girl once more, comforted and protected by the awkward boy who was her only friend. "*Kuso,*" she muttered, relaxing into his embrace.

"What does that mean?"

"Shite, in Eastshyre."

Graham's chuckle rumbled against her chest. He pushed her away and called for one of his men to toss him an apple. "Show me what that thing can do." He threw the fruit high into the air.

With the briefest of movements, Jiliana brought her *katana* up in an arc, slicing through the apple in a single deadly stroke.

To her complete astonishment, Graham caught the two

halves as they fell, gazing at them with a fierce smile. "Not bad at all. I have never seen a cut so clean." He bit into one half and handed her the other. "So, do you want the bloody job?" He turned to stride toward the group of men still gaping at them. "If you do, be here at dawn."

Dawn it would be, Jiliana thought with a completely inappropriate satisfaction as she bit into her half of the sweet and juicy fruit.

"Can I ask you a question?" He handed his own sword off to one of his men, giving her a final look over his shoulder. "Why on earth do you want to be a squire?"

What could she tell him that he would understand? "Because I intend to be the first female knight in all of Westmyre," she answered, hoping he wouldn't search further for the truth.

"Of course." He smacked his forehead and rolled his eyes. "I should have known it all along."

Chapter Two

Graham clenched his fists as the prince regent—disguised as a knight called Sir Bertram—glared at him from atop his massive destrier. "Care to go again, *Duncemore*," the braggart taunted, raising his visor to give Jili a dazzling smile.

"Sir Duncemore," Graham corrected stupidly, taking an involuntary step toward the princeling. But his squire grabbed his arm, wrapping her fingers hard around the blood-soaked sleeve of his gambeson, the sting of pain enough to clear the fog of fury from his mind.

"Sir Graham," she said respectfully, "we must tend to your wound."

Graham hesitated. No one, not even he, was supposed to know who the prince was, and it wouldn't take more than a single punch to knock the wanker off his horse and show him who was the better man here. It would do the prince good, he thought belligerently, to have his nose broken at least once.

Sir Bertram's eyes gleamed as if he realized Graham's intent. Was that an unspoken challenge in their depths? Of course there was, he realized, when the man's gaze moved to Jili once more.

Graham's unusual choice of a squire had most definitely caused the uproar he'd expected...but instead of ridiculing him for his decision, it seemed that every damned knight on the field was doing his best to lure her from his side. And he would never let that happen. Not even if Jili herself agreed to the match.

Hellfire! Graham shook his head. He was acting like some jealous suitor trying to keep her all for himself. Jili was a grown woman, a fully trained warrior capable of making her own decision.

He cursed his mothers for the thousandth time as the prince dropped from his horse. Bertram was tall, Graham acknowledged, assessing the other man. With a decent girth to his shoulder and arms thickly knotted with muscle. It wasn't often Graham met anyone who could give him a fitting challenge, either on or off the field. The princeling could, and that thought made his hackles rise.

Especially when the braggart took Jili's hand and brought it to his lips. "If you ever get tired of this dullard and want to work for a real man—"

When Graham snorted in derision, Bertram ignored the rude sound.

"—you know where to find me," he continued as if he and Jili were all alone.

She politely pulled her hand away and wiped it on her *hakama*—what she had said her wide-legged pants were called. "I'll be certain to add you to the list." Dismissing him entirely, she turned to Graham. "'Tis time, master."

He gaped at her in shock, concealing the expression quickly. Master was it? Although he knew it was said strictly for the other man's benefit, Graham had trouble swallowing down his thrill at her use of the title.

He'd lain awake many a night these past few weeks, lost in stupid fantasies of having her offer him more personal services, and her calling him master fit right in with his idiotic musings.

His cock roused and Graham bit back a groan, forcing the thoughts away. They had a purely professional relationship, he reminded himself—again. Jili's past made anything else impossible. He would do nothing to betray her trust.

Giving the prince a smug smile, he followed her as she hurried ahead. When he finally entered their tent, he swore. The jousting had not gone well at all. Bertram had made a far better show than expected, the arrogant bastard almost unseating him before Graham finally won the match. But he'd taken a decent shot to the shoulder and a thick splinter of wood from the prince's javelin had rammed itself beneath his arm.

And this was only the first day of the competition in a tournament—that for whatever stupid reason the earl sponsoring it had decided—was supposed to last seven days.

Graham threw his helmet into the corner. "I fully intend to kill him."

Jili motioned two serving boys to set a bath up near the bed. "Got you, did he?" She untied his cuirass and eased it off. "He always strikes low to the left. Why haven't you figured that out by now?" She knelt before him and untied his chausses.

"I didn't ask for a replay of the event." He glowered down at her.

Her grin was amused. "Then you should have. 'Tis my duty to keep you informed of your opponent's weaknesses. While you might believe he's an ass—"

"Prince Ass, actually."

Both her brows disappeared beneath her bangs. "Indeed?"

"But he doesn't know that I know, and you are definitely not supposed to know. Hell," Graham added with a shake of his head. "I don't even know what I'm talking about."

What he said next was far from polite as he tried to pull the quilted gambeson over his head, wincing when it caught on the wood. "Can you see it?" Jili ran cool fingers over his skin as she stood to inspect the injury. She smelled exotic, of jasmine and other imported flowers, the foreign scents stirring his overly deprived senses.

They'd been training together for four long weeks, and in all that time, for whatever stupid reason, Graham had stayed with her every night, aching and unrelieved. He hadn't gone this long without a woman since before he'd topped his very first. And despite his best efforts, the strain was beginning to show. Not that he'd even begun to admit his fantasies all centered around his squire, and that even the thought of a paid companion made his gut roll. When in the hell had Jili become the center of all his needs?

He'd pictured her in a thousand different positions, on her back, on her stomach, on her knees...on his knees. His flesh roused as the familiar images began to play out in his mind. And now, as she studied his arm, with her face so close to his neck he could feel her breath, Graham's frustrations rose to new and more desperate levels. He squirmed, trying to ease the growing pressure in his breeches.

"Hold still," Jili ordered. "This is quite a big piece." Wrapping a cloth around the wood, she gave a hard jerk, pulling out the sliver in a single easy move.

Graham grunted. At least the pain in his arm took his mind off the ache of his cock. "Stitches?"

She wiped the blood away. "Perhaps one or two. Should I call the *chirurgeon* or do it myself?"

"Just do it and get it over with." Graham sat down and held out his feet. Jili knelt and pulled off his boots. "I stink," he said as the foul odor rose up to fill the air.

Her laugh was easy. "Badly. If you want, I can work on

your arm while you bathe."

It was the first time she had ever offered to be present while he bathed. Not that he'd done it very often lately.

Although he opened his mouth to refuse her offer, he was so tired and smelled so bad, Graham decided to take the risk. He wasn't certain how Jili would react, and if she fled in embarrassment, he would know not to do it again. In truth, he'd deliberately avoided this situation, knowing that each night when he sponged himself off, she turned her face away until he was clothed again.

Her past still haunted her, of that he had no doubts.

When at last he nodded, she left the tent and barked orders to the younger boys. He smiled at the tone in her voice. She could be downright bossy when she wanted to. The tub was filled quickly. Throwing caution to the wind, Graham stripped and sank into the bath. Jili pulled the footstool over and laid out the needle and thread.

"Do we really have to do that?" Graham felt his nerves stretch. While he could take whatever pain was inflicted on him in battle or the tournament, the idea of letting her calmly stick a needle into his flesh was nauseating. He'd passed out on more than one occasion while getting sewn up in the past, and really didn't want to make a fool of himself now.

"Are you chicken?" A grin tilted up one corner of her mouth.

"If you must know," he answered truthfully, feeling the dull red flush creeping up his neck, "yes." Graham tried to relax against the side of the tub as the hot water loosened the tension from his muscles. He sighed in contentment just before Jili stuck the needle deep into his arm.

Graham swore and jumped, splashing water everywhere,

causing Jiliana to yank hard on the thread. "Baby," she scolded him, tying off the knot, studying her work to make certain she hadn't pulled the stitch free.

"Damn, woman, are you trying to kill me?" He blinked at her through long dark lashes, the weariness in his eyes clearly visible.

"Just one more," she promised, wanting to stroke the pain from his face. "I'll be quick." And she was. In seconds she had finished and Graham relaxed again with a heavy sigh of relief.

"You can go get something to eat," he mumbled, his eyes drifting shut. "I plan on staying here until the water gets so cold I can't stand it, then I'm going straight to bed. I have to face that damned prince again on the morrow."

But Jiliana was unwilling to leave. More and more often, she found herself wanting to stay in his company no matter where they were. She could think of nothing she'd rather do than run her hands over his shoulders, knead the ache from his muscles, and hear him whisper her name in grateful surrender. She was drawn to him as heaven to earth, yin to yang, darkness to light.

Her thoughts shocked her as a thrill of desire rippled through her body. Needs she had long since locked away begged her for release, their dangerous ache filling her with both anticipation and a deep seated dread.

Forcing down the memories that surfaced with the want, Jiliana dunked a cloth in the water and very carefully cleaned the blood from Graham's arm. She stared at his body in fascination, noting the breadth of his shoulders and the hard plane of his stomach. She even let her gaze linger on the mass of flesh that bobbed between his thighs.

She frowned as regret worked its way into her heart, her memories coming too close for comfort. *Terror. Pain. The sound of her own voice screaming. The sound of newer voices adding their cries to the chaos.* With a force of will she brought herself back to the present.

If her life had been different, she acknowledged in unaccustomed sorrow, she could have been pledged to a man like Graham, feeling his body against hers in the night...hearing him call her name in affection, tasting his mouth when he kissed her. And there were still so many things he didn't know. So many mistakes made in the years that stood between them. What man could ever come to love a woman who had done the things she had?

Not that she expected love, or any emotion that came close to it. She had locked those dreams away in the prison of her mind. *Desire has a heavy price,* the masters had taught her. *To want too much is like trying to catch the wind.*

But tonight, when he was so strangely vulnerable and injured, she couldn't make herself leave him. "At least let me wash your hair," she heard herself say, moving the stool to sit behind him. She dipped the cloth in the tub once more and dripped water over his head and shoulders.

After she found the bar of soap and worked up a decent lather, her fingers dug into his scalp as she worked the soap through his hair and down his neck, applying a good amount of pressure to the tensely knotted muscles. When her hands began to tire, she used her elbows and forearms.

He sighed again, one corner of his mouth turning up. "I hope that arrogant asshole doesn't get such good treatment from his squire," he said smugly. "I'll best him easily."

She snorted. "Not if you don't remember where he strikes. You let him hit you every time today." She rinsed off the soap and moved to sit at Graham's side, lathering his chest and working down across his stomach. The mass between his legs stirred, grew and hardened to an impressive length. She found her fingers trailing closer and closer as the desire to touch him spiraled out of control.

Without warning, Graham's hand clamped tight around her wrist. "'Tis enough. That is not a squire's job."

Her gaze flew to his face. While his jaw was clenched and his lips were pressed tight together, he hadn't opened his eyes. She knew he had deliberately kept them shut, sparing her any embarrassment. "'Tis for some," she argued stubbornly.

He chuckled, still not looking at her. "Agreed, but not for you. Go to sleep, Jili, we have a long day tomorrow."

"You haven't been with a woman since—" Jiliana drew her brows together "—since I have been here," she said as the realization struck. They had been together night and day.

He grunted, bringing her wrist to his cheek. "I can take care of it myself once you have gone."

"What if I wanted to?" She did not know what possessed her to make the offer, but as soon as she said the words, she realized the truth. She wanted to wrap her hands around his shaft and have him teach her how to please him.

This time his eyes shot open. "Not a good idea."

"Why not?" The more he refused her, the more she determined she became. "Would it be so horrible to have me touch you?"

He dropped her wrist and ran a hand through his short-cropped hair. It stood up in wet spikes, making him look more desirable than before. Jiliana's body flamed again, the ache spreading from between her legs to race across her stomach. The sensation was unlike any she had felt before. It begged to be acknowledged, demanded not to be ignored.

"If I said I wanted to...us to...I mean, what if we

could...Graham, I am a grown woman and I've never done anything since—" She broke off and lowered her head, the flush of shame rising fast into her cheeks. Maybe he was right. Maybe she shouldn't push for more.

To her surprise he tucked a finger beneath her chin and forced her to meet his gaze. "You know I would never do anything to hurt you."

She nodded, swallowing around the dryness of her throat.

"And you can trust me."

She nodded again.

"Are you sure this is what you want?" His eyes held such a serious look she reached out to smooth her hand across his cheek. "Oh, hell, Jili," he muttered, wrapping his hand around her neck and pulling her face to his. "I know I will regret this," he whispered, rising from the tub in a shower of water to stand naked and wanting before her, "but I don't have the will to say no."

Grabbing a cloth, he briefly dried himself before taking her hand and leading her to the bed. When she hesitated, he gave her a gentle look. "Say the word and we stop. No matter what...no matter when. Agreed?"

Jiliana knew the blush covered her from head to toe, but she met his gaze as boldly as she could. "Would you not touch me...not yet?"

"If you tell me not to." Graham sat on the edge of the bed and pulled her down beside him.

The warmth of him surrounded her, the smell of him clean and sharp in her nose. She had nearly forgotten how big he was when he had been folded up in the tiny tub, but now, faced with the full force of the man, his size alone was almost enough to make her change her mind.

Almost.

Had she not known what a gentle giant he truly was, she might have fled in fear, but Graham had always been her friend, and he had proven his honor on a daily basis. While forever was not an option, this night was, and she intended to make the most of it. Why not? What would it cost her in the end? A heart could only hold so much pain. Hers was full, she was safe.

"Tell me how to please you," she whispered, dropping her hand on one huge thigh. When he jumped, she smiled softly. She had the power here, she was in control. The thought calmed her even as it fueled her longing. "Um, do you think you could lie down and put your hands behind your head?"

He complied with alacrity, completely comfortable in his skin as he stretched out on the bed and did as she asked, his arms bulging as he bent them, wincing only once when the stitches pulled too tight.

"Wait." Jiliana shook her head, not wanting the wound to open again. Pulling a lacing from his discarded shirt, she opted for a different plan. "Put your wrists together."

He chuckled, a deep and glorious sound. "Do you really plan to tie me up?" A darker expression flickered across his face.

Jiliana nodded, nibbling at her lip. She watched in fascination as his cock swelled, demanding that she touch him. And she would touch him...over and over and over through the night.

"I think I could learn to like this game." His voice roughened as she tied off the knot.

"So could I," she answered, her own voice shaky and uncertain. "Now what should I do?" But before he could answer, she was already running her hands down his stomach, reveling in the feel of his skin sliding beneath hers. She grew bolder and splayed her hands on the inside of his thighs, exploring the quivering muscles there, moving unerringly toward the prize that jutted proudly toward her.

The sting between her own legs grew, blocking out every thought except for Graham, this moment, and the mantle of need that wrapped them together. With a sigh of contentment she finally took him in her hands, the pillar of flesh feeling as thick and smooth as she'd imagined.

"In the east," she managed to say, "this is called the jade scepter." And she felt as if she'd found such a royal treasure as she rubbed Graham's flesh between her palms.

Graham bit off a moan as Jili finally wrapped her fingers around him, smoothing them over his cock. Mesmerized by the sight of her, the feel of her, he studied every line and angle of her face as she stroked him slowly, from root to tip and back again. His hips bucked involuntarily against her hand, and he did his best to make no other move to hurry her...but it was growing more difficult by the second.

He'd never really expected, in all the nights he'd lain awake picturing it, that his fantasy might actually come true Was this how his brothers felt when they first met the women they would come to love?

Love? He bit back another moan as she curled both hands around his cock. Oh, no, they were not going there. If she wanted him to help her learn about pleasure, that was fine. He was a generous man, more than willing to comply, as any true gentleman would. And when they were finished they could walk away. No guilt...no regret.

He sucked in his breath as she reached between his legs and cupped his heavy sac.

"Shite, Jili," he gritted out after several long minutes. "I don't know how much longer I can hold out." His hands strained against the bindings, his fingers clenching and unclenching in rhythm to her strokes. He wanted to touch her, teach her, do something other than lay there in silence, but he knew she wasn't ready yet. The image of her held close in his arms as he reached out to lick one perfect tipped breast, or use his fingers to stroke her clit before driving his cock deep and high into the silken heat of her—

"Faster," he ordered, staring her straight in the eye as the rush of release began. "Harder," he added, his jaw pulsing in urgency.

"Like this?" Jili did as he demanded, speeding up her strokes and clenching her fingers tighter around him. She stopped once to explore the drop of seed that spilled from the tip of his cock, spreading the moisture down along his shaft, and Graham thought he would die as she slowed the pace again.

His hips bucked, the tension visible for both of them to see. "Ahhhhhhh, 'tis good Jili," he said when she pumped him faster. "Look at me. I want you to see how much I want—"

Their eyes met and held. Graham's entire body shook as she finally pushed him over the edge. He jerked hard against her hand as the pleasure overtook him, every nerve and muscle working in perfect unison as he lost control, whispering her name like some love-addled ass as he shot his seed high onto his chest.

He heard his guttural cries of release and wondered at the urgent sound, already wishing he had not come so soon, dreading the moment when she would pull her hands away. *Not yet*, he wanted to beg. *Keep touching me. Or let me touch you and I will never ever stop.*

In confusion, he swallowed down the words. No Dunmore begged a woman for more. It just wasn't done! At least not by Graham Dunmore, he added, letting his eyes close and his head sink back against the bed. He'd heard Llew and Allard beg their wives on numerous occasions.

Damn it, damn it, damn it! This wasn't working out at all like he'd originally thought. Her simple request for education was turning into a needy and complicated matter.

"Graham?" Her voice broke into the chaos of his mind. It was soft, shy, a growing embarrassment coloring her tone. "Was that...are you...did I do that right?" A wash of blood suffused her cheeks and she lowered her lashes, refusing to look him directly in the eye. Graham cursed to himself again and raised his hands to cup her face.

"Perfect." He planted what he intended to be a brotherly kiss on her cheek, but when she turned to face him, their lips met instead.

Before he could stop himself, he pulled her face closer, slanting his mouth over hers as he let the kiss deepen. To his astonishment she did not draw away. When her lips opened slightly and her breath came out in a whimper, Graham realized something he should have noticed long before. She was fumbling in a state of arousal she had no way to control or release, her hips squirming restlessly against his thigh, her fingers tugging urgently at the leather that still bound his hands.

Desire hit hard and fast once more. Despite the fact she'd just relieved him, her desperate want sent his own hunger higher. "Jili," he mouthed against her lips. "I could—"

But already she was coiling back into herself, wrapping the years of protection around her. "I can't." She shook her head, her gaze flickering to his newly stiffened cock. "Not *that*," she finished, closing her eyes as she turned her face away.

When he was a boy, Graham had not fully understood the enormity of what she had lost when she had been attacked. As a man, he finally saw the truth. His fury rose like the clouds before a storm. But not at her...he would never fault her for an instant.

"Untie my hands," he said. "There are many things I could show you...many ways to please you."

Her fingers stopped, the knot remaining firmly tied, her hesitation a wall between them.

"You could even keep your clothes on," Graham heard himself add. *Shut up*, he ordered silently, as his mouth continued to run. "I swear I would never do anything to hurt you."

Tangling his fingers in her hair, he tilted her face up to his. Her eyes were huge in the candle-light, flickers of shadow deepening their hue, turning their color from grey to black and back again.

Graham finally forced himself to silence. He'd made the offer. He could do nothing more.

Jiliana trembled when she caught the look of hunger etched across Graham's face. On another man it would have sent her running for her *katana*. On another man it would have made her shudder in fear. But Graham's expression made her want him to wrap her in the strength of his arms and never let her go.

The temptation was brutal. She couldn't resist. "If I don't like it we can stop anytime? You swear?"

They had played this game before, she remembered with a

catch in her heart as she held up her pinkie. Graham encircled it with his own, the huge finger dwarfing hers.

He nodded solemnly.

"And I can keep all my clothes on?"

"Every stitch."

She wanted to make some joke, tell some ribald story to break the odd mood that had settled between them, but her mouth would not form the words, her mind refusing to think of anything but how it would feel to have Graham touch her.

"Done," she whispered.

"Done," Graham repeated. He stretched out beside her on the bed, his head propped on one folded arm, smiling ruefully when she wiped his chest off with a cloth. He studied her for long moments and she grew disconcerted beneath the heavy weight of his gaze.

As she opened her mouth to protest, he reached out and trailed his fingers across her cheek, letting them linger on the scar that cut across her jaw before tugging on a lock of her hair.

"Ever been well and truly kissed?" When she shook her head, his grin grew sinful. "Okay then, what an excellent place to start."

The tug on her hair grew more insistent, dragging her head toward his. When his mouth connected solidly with hers, Jiliana's world melted like ice in the sun. The desire she had felt before paled to embers beside the fire that burned inside her now. Graham pulled her beside him, positioning her so that every inch of her body was cradled by every inch of his. His cock swelled against her stomach, giving her a momentary shiver of alarm, but as his lips slid over hers and his hand cupped her chin, she gave herself over to the wonder of it all.

Until she realized that instead of easing the brutal ache

that gripped her body, his kiss was making the agony grow. When she opened her mouth to tell him so in no uncertain terms, he thrust his tongue between her lips, this new invasion wringing a desperate whimper from her throat.

Jiliana wasn't stupid, nor had she spent her life locked away in the church. She'd seen people kiss, even watched them couple furtively in dark alleys and shadowed corners, turning away in disgust when her memories pressed too close. But she'd never felt anything that remotely resembled this shock of need that swept up from her stomach. The burn between her legs slammed over her in waves, reaching, waiting, grasping desperately for something she could barely put a name to.

His tongue teased hers, slid in and back again. Jiliana let her own tongue explore, writhing in a sweep of bliss when Graham sucked it deep into his mouth. They challenged and warred with each other, each strike and parry measured to make the other tremble and shake.

When he dragged his mouth away, she buried her face in his neck, unwilling to let him see how far she had already fallen. He rolled her over on her back, his breath as harsh and labored as hers. "You learn fast," he gritted out.

The pleased sound that bubbled up from her chest ended in a gasp as Graham's hand closed around her breast. What torture had he devised to torment her with now? When he found her nipple and rolled it gently between his fingers, Jiliana jumped, her cry of need hanging harsh in the air between them.

"Shhhhhh," he whispered, pinching harder, making her scream again.

"Ahhhhhh." She sucked in her breath as a new madness overtook her. Despite her earlier admonitions, she now wanted to rip off every piece of clothing she wore and feel his skin against hers.

But he had yet to do the thing he promised. Instead of easing her need, so far he had only driven it higher. The pain shot deep into her body, causing an unfamiliar emptiness.

"Please, Graham," she begged, ashamed of the desperation she heard in her tone. "*Please.*" She ground her hips insistently against his, hoping something would soothe the overwhelming ache.

One of his hands slid down her stomach to nudge apart her thighs, settling heavy between them. For the briefest instant the old fear rose up, but in the rush of her need, it was quickly forgotten.

Burrowing his fingers into the folds of her flesh, Graham began to rub a spot that was far more sensitive than the others. "What do they call this in Eastshyre?" he demanded.

"The g-golden p-p-pearl." Jiliana's cries grew louder as he pressed the knot between his fingers, teasing the tender spot until she thought the pain would never end. Deep inside her body the emptiness cried out, the long years of aloneness demanding to be filled. She wiggled against Graham's hand, praying his touch would soothe her soon.

She was reaching for something...some place she'd never imagined, and she could feel herself creeping closer to the edge, tottering on the brink, ready to fall, ready to float, but she could not fling herself over the line to the bliss that waited in the other side.

"Jili." Graham's voice was concerned as he drew back to look at her. "'Tis all right to let go. I promise to catch you." He deepened the pressure between her legs, his fingers finding her cunt and nudging just a bit inside, as far as the material of her *hakama* would allow.

Jiliana knew what she wanted. What she had to have to make her pleasure complete. Graham inside her...his fingers parting her body, filling her, taking her. She pulled his face to hers. "This is not enough," she whimpered against his mouth.

Graham captured her lips in another kiss as he bent her knee and draped her leg over his. He slid his hand inside one leg of her *hakama*, the feel of his skin against hers driving her hunger even higher.

"Is this what you need?" he demanded.

She nodded, mutely. His hand slid higher, coming to rest just beside the juncture of her thigh. "And this?"

She nodded again, unable to speak, wanting nothing more than to feel his mouth hard on hers and his fingers thrust inside her. Despite all her earlier cautions and despite her earlier hesitation, she wanted—needed—to feel Graham reach high into her body, soothing the space that waited so ready for his touch.

"Inside me," she said. "I want to feel you—" Her words ended in a whimper as Graham nudged a thick finger into her body.

Jiliana was totally unprepared for the sensation. Her sex clamped hard around his finger, too tight, too untrained. She cried his name in a voice she did not recognize, barely registering the fact that the entire camp had probably heard her scream, wanting to tell him to stop, wanting to tell him to give her even more.

"What is this called, Jili?"

"*Graham.* Ummm....I...ahhhhhhh—the gate of jewels." Her words ended in a cry that Graham smothered with his mouth, breaching her lips with his tongue as his finger plunged into her again. Her arms curled around his neck, her own fingers digging in his hair as he continued this urgent assault, taking her over and over with his hand until the pleasure built to an unbearable pitch.

The calloused pad of his thumb swirled around the swollen flesh of her golden pearl, the added sensation almost more than she could take. He urged his finger higher into her body, opening her wider, taking her deeper than he had before, the shock of the stretch causing her flesh to clench around him as the pleasure fought against the sting of his invasion.

"Mmmmmmmmmmm, unmmmmmmmmmmm," came the muffled sounds of her confusion as she shook like the untried maiden that she was.

"Come for me, little one," Graham whispered. With a long and final thrust, he buried his finger inside her, stroking the thick wall of muscle until she thought she would die from the touch. "Scream for me again."

At long last the pleasure surfaced, dragging the scream from her throat as her desire blossomed into a rush of fire that Jiliana could not hold at bay. She came for the first time in her life, her body shaking in glorious abandon as Graham continued to invade the secret chamber of her sex.

His kiss deepened, gentled, deepened again, and she soon became aware of the insistent thrusting of his hips against hers. Without a single thought of shame, she reached between them and took his cock in her hand, pumping him hard and fast as his fingers continued to pump inside her.

Already the ache was building once more, taking her breath away as the sensation soared again. The second wave was smaller, easier, made all the sweeter by the sound of Graham's voice as he groaned his pleasure against her mouth. The steel of his flesh rode fast in her hand, its mass an already familiar weight as she stroked him to completion.

When he finally pulled his finger free, Jiliana fought back the urge to order him to stop as she felt the heat of him withdraw. "Lesson one completed," he mumbled in a shaky voice, tucking her head onto his chest. "I hope I survive lesson two."

She braved a glance at him from between her lashes. "What do you mean?" Embarrassment already tried to wedge itself between them. The all too familiar emotion brought with it an unexpected rush of tears. Warriors did not cry. Not if they wanted to survive.

"I mean...damn it, I don't know what I mean, only that I have never known a woman to come with such utter abandon," he stated with a growl. "'Twas not an insult," he added, when she stiffened and tried to pull away.

"I already said I won't let you bed me properly," she protested, plucking aimlessly at her shirt. "So, obviously there will be no other lessons."

His laughter rolled across her ears. "There are many other things I can show you without ever topping you properly. That is, if you are still willing to learn."

His stomach growled and hers answered. To her surprise she found she was ravenously hungry...and thoroughly intrigued by Graham's bold statement.

Oh yes, she wanted another lesson. And another, and another. But as the aftermath settled between them, she didn't know if she dared.

She untangled herself from Graham's embrace and stood, straightening her clothing. She tried her best not to stare as he rose and dressed himself, but it was hard to keep her gaze away. The man was an irresistible force. Would she be the unmoving object he fought, or was it time for her to finally learn to flow like wind and water?

Either way, her thoughts were cut short by the shouts of alarm stirring up the camp. The heavy clank of weaponry filled the evening, the sounds of people screaming as they ran to see the sight. "Someone has been killed! An animal attack!"

Chapter Three

Jiliana stared at the mangled body of the young man in a pool of his own blood. All around her people grumbled, crossing themselves while muttering half-forgotten prayers and stories of human-eating monsters they had heard when they were children.

She watched in forced detachment, refusing to be drawn into the scene, until an odd and elusive scent drifted past on an evening breeze, fading too fast for her fully catch. Nevertheless, she scanned the area intently, all her senses alert and on guard.

A single beggar hobbled mournfully down the road, leaning on a crooked stick. Two or three children ran screaming for their mothers, scared silly by the sight of the dead man's body and the ever growing tales whispered by the rest of the crowd. A flock of garishly dressed women waited in the background, posing lewdly in search of their night's wages...or at least enough to buy a decent meal.

Nothing seemed out of the ordinary. Nothing looked the slightest bit out of place. Another reason to keep wary and alert.

"What's the matter?" Graham stepped close so only she could hear, his gaze casually following the line of hers.

"Have you ever known any animal in Westmyre to make claw-marks like that?" She nodded at the long gouges dug deep into the man's chest. "And isn't he one of Bertram's guards?"

Graham's head shot up as he reached for his sword. "Yes. I recognize his colors."

Jiliana let her own hand rest on the hilt of her *katana.* "They are saying 'tis a wolf attack—a demon-wolf attack," she added mockingly. "But wolves bite...not claw. Do you see one bite mark anywhere on him?"

By this time Bertram had pushed his way through the crowd. "Get back to whatever you were doing," he shouted at the group of gawking onlookers. "You don't have to be afraid. My men and I will track the animal down and have its pelt for you to see by morning."

Jiliana frowned. Some innocent creature was going to pay for a crime it hadn't committed. The thought made her sick to her stomach. Her years in the east had taught her a tolerance and appreciation for the natural world that most in Westmyre did not share. There was always too much killing.

She gave Bertram a challenging look. "How will you know you have gotten the right one, and not just the first you stumble on in order to calm the fears of the crowd?"

He looked back at her calmly. "Because our very own Sir Graham is going to lead the hunt. Isn't that right, Duncemore?"

Jiliana felt Graham stiffen beside her and cursed her stupid mouth. But his tone was placid when he answered.

"I would be honored." He pointed to several lesser knights. "You four will join me. Saddle your mounts. There is no time to waste." He made certain she saw the irritation simmering in his eyes as he turned to leave.

She cursed to herself. Her rash statement would cost him hours of sleep—and he had a full schedule in the lists tomorrow, facing Bertram in sword combat at the very end of the day. By night-fall he would be well past exhausted. And not likely to forgive her if he slipped down in the rankings. So much for her plan to be the best squire ever.

She stayed as the crowd dispersed and the man's body was removed. By now it was so dark she could barely see a thing except for the lights from the camp behind, and the string of torches in the distance as Graham led his group in search of an enemy that wasn't there.

The scene ran over and over in her mind, and though Jiliana could find no reason for her growing agitation, her worries would not be stilled. She slept little that night, tossing and turning on Graham's cot alone.

Graham returned near daybreak, so furious and frustrated he could have gladly wrung the prince's neck. "We did not find a thing," he said, flinging himself onto the bed. "Not one damned wolf in the entire damned forest!" He ran a hand through his hair and stared into space. "You should have seen the smug look on Bertram's face when I had to tell him we failed. Leave them," he added when Jili tugged at one of his boots. "I'll just have to put them back on in a blasted minute anyway."

She sat on her heels and cocked her head. "I am sorry. I should have kept my thoughts to myself."

"Damned right, you should have." But already his anger was fading. It really wasn't her fault. Someone had to go after the beast. Graham figured Bertram would have picked him, anyway—the ass. And the only reason he'd agreed was because he knew Bertram was really the prince, and that both his royal parents had hired Graham to protect him. This was all part of the job—lousy one that it was.

But if either of his two mothers—or the prince's—thought

he would ever agree to this again...they all had a big surprise waiting.

"Just bring me some food and a good strong cup of tea. And add a slug of Derbyn brandy," he called after her as she ducked out the door. He was going need the burn of the drink to get him up and running...especially if Jili was right and there was more to this death than met the eye.

After seeing Graham settled as best she could, Jiliana walked to a nearby field and faced the rising sun, letting her breath slow and her mind still. It would be a glorious day, she thought, watching the light sneak up to chase away the dark. She frowned, the peace she sought so desperately vanishing along with the twinkling of the stars.

The sight of the youth's mutilated body refused to be pushed away. It had been a far from pleasant death for one so very young. Not that she hadn't seen more than her share of death, in all its many guises. The masters taught that wisdom came from acceptance, but she often wondered if acceptance was just another word for apathy. A way to excuse one's actions and pretend it was necessary as she had done on more than one occasion. Could you be so detached from life you lost sight of its greater meaning?

The voice of her teacher whispered in amusement. "One must learn to accept the unacceptable. Change cannot be avoided or refused. Only in this truth can one hope to find freedom."

She stood, shaking her doubts aside. She would find no peace today.

Better to work the body than let the mind take over. She assumed the proper stance and began the first movement, resting her weight on her back leg while bending the other and touching the point of her toe on the ground.

"What are you doing?" She jumped at Graham's husky voice, her frustration rising as her calmness was again disrupted.

"It's called a *kata*." She glowered up at him, refusing to be pacified by how adorable he looked. His hair stuck out in all directions and he yawned, scratching his armpits.

Graham circled a finger in the air. "Show me."

To her utter chagrin, Jiliana became suddenly shy under the scrutiny of his sharp blue eyes. But if he truly wanted to learn, she was obligated to teach him. This was how it had always been.

She assumed her earlier position. "Each posture is a strike or blow, performed slowly with the utmost precision and concentration." She shifted her weight to her front leg, sweeping her arms across her body as she turned to face the other direction. She brought her hands up and clawed her fingers. "Tiger."

Graham copied her, surprising her again with the grace of his movements.

"Very good," she told him, taking a large step forward to crouch close to the ground. Her fingers touched into a pointed strike. "Snake."

Graham said nothing as he mimicked her once more. Jiliana stood, her hands held high with the fingers pointing down. "Crane."

For long moments they moved silently together; teacher and student, master and squire. Her earlier restlessness calmed as the joy of the *kata* took over. Graham proved a quick study, and when they had finished, he looked at her with a new appreciation.

"Do you do this every day?"

"Yes."

"And you will teach me?"

She placed her palms together and gave him an assessing look. "Once the training has begun, you must be willing to follow it through to the end. The student and master both have obligations."

He nodded, moving close to caress her cheek. His grin could have made the devil blush. "Shall we consider it an even trade?" She felt her skin prickle when he ran his tongue across his teeth and pulled her hard against him. The mood between them grew heavy with lush and sinful needs.

Until his stomach rumbled loudly. His roar of laughter echoed across the field. "But a man must have his priorities straight. Break our fast first...then I plan on showing that damned Bertram just who is the better man."

Jiliana frowned at his boastful words. "Not if you don't remember he strikes low and to the left. I'll have my needle waiting just in case.

"Low and to the left," Graham was mumbling when he returned to his tent at the end of the day. "Low and to the left." He threw his helmet into a corner. "Who in the bloody hell holds a week long tournament, anyway? Doesn't the damned earl know these things are only supposed to last two days?"

Graham swore as Jili began to stitch up the gash along his forearm. He was furious with both her and the damned princeling. "Low and to the left," he bellowed, sending Jili into a fit of laughter which she hurriedly stifled.

"That was the lance, Sir Graham," she managed to say in a decently placating tone. "Today you met him on the sparring field. He aims to the right with his broadsword."

Graham frowned at the silk of her hair. It fell against her cheek as she worked. He fingered a lock of it in his other hand, its softness soothing as she pricked him again with the needle. "I swear, woman, if not for my sworn duty to the queen—"

"I know, I know, you would put the braggart in his place." Jili tied off the last stitch and sat back, admiring her work. "Done. I could get you some willow bark tea to take the sting away."

Graham stood and shook his head. "I have a much better idea." He shrugged into his shirt, his mood lifting with every second. "How about we have a few drinks and I can teach you another thing or two?" Without waiting for her answer, he hauled her against him, reveling in the feel of her body pressed so close to his. His breath caught when her eyes met his and he saw the longing fighting to the surface.

"I haven't cleaned your armor yet."

"Turn it over to one of the younger boys. They need the practice."

"Nor have I washed your gambeson."

"'Twill do for another day."

"And your sword is not polished or sharpened."

He let his smile grow lecherous. "But you can take care of that before the night is over, Jili."

A wash of color climbed up her cheeks as she realized his meaning. "Are you certain I shouldn't turn that over to one of the boys as well?" She raised one lovely eyebrow.

He laughed and crushed her even closer. "Come. I need food, wine...and you," he added softly against her cheek, letting his thumb trace the scar across her jaw. He was fascinated with the mark. Its jagged line made the rest of her features seem delicate in comparison.

In truth, she was a study in oppositions—one of the most well-trained warriors he had ever met, and one of the most beautiful women he had ever seen. Her dual natures fascinated him as she rubbed her cheek against his hand and grasped the hilt of her deadly blade.

"It has been quiet so far today, but that doesn't mean it will stay that way."

Graham nodded and reached for his own sword-belt, reluctantly letting her step away. "Agreed. So maybe we'll have more food than drink...until we retire for the night."

Although Jili blushed again, she didn't say no, he realized with a growing hunger. His cock roused in anticipation, his mind already lost in visions of new ways to please her.

The camp was still awash in activity as they walked to the makeshift square in its center. Jili let Graham walk in front of her as was her duty, but he would have much rather had her at his side, their hands clasped and fingers entwined.

Bloody hell. When had he become such a sentimental idiot? Holding hands. Only the very old or young held hands. Real men had no time for such silly gestures. The thought, however, didn't comfort him as it should have when they reached the buildings set up to serve food.

"Who is that?" Jili tipped her head to where an elegantly dressed man chatted and laughed with an unruly group of knights as she and Graham approached.

"Earl Rulfert come to mingle with the common man." Graham watched him through narrowed eyes. "Richer than the crown, or so I've heard, and he makes no effort to hide the fact. 'Twas his idea to host the tournament, his money that pays the champion."

The earl bellowed for wine and ale and entertainment. The evening erupted with cheers as the square filled to capacity. Musicians vied for a place near where he sat, hats and scarves laid out for whatever money he cared to throw them. Dancers settled in like a mob of crows, slinking over the men in the hopes to earn more than the price of a dance while merchants wrote down how much drink was consumed in order to collect when the revelries were through.

"His castle sits just beyond the forest." Graham nodded toward the line of trees. "You won't find him sleeping on a cot or the ground. Damn, he's seen us." Unable to get out of the obligation, he led Jili to where Rulfert presided over the square as if he was the king.

"Sir Graham." Rulfert held out his hand to be kissed.

Graham took it with distaste, but did as he was bid. It was never prudent to make enemies of those above you. "Your Grace. What an honor to see you here."

"And is this the squire I have heard so much about?" His eyes slithered to Jili as Graham dropped his hand.

"This is Jiliana."

The earl motioned her forward. "I have heard tales of her beauty and fighting skills. I can see they weren't exaggerated." He held out his hand for her to kiss.

She took it gracefully, bowing low to admire the rings that circled every one of his puffy fingers. "You have been to Eastshyre, Your Grace?"

A younger man stepped between them, taking Jili's hand and touching it to his lips. "Lord Reginald Blenham at your service. My uncle has never stepped one foot out of Westmyre. What made you ask?"

Graham did his best to be polite. He had never met the earl's nephew, and while he had formed no judgment of the man, he didn't like the way he was looking at Jili as if she was intended for his midnight snack. If she was going to be anybody's snack, Graham had placed his order first.

Jili shook her head and stepped away, her own smile perfectly settled into place. "I just thought that a man of your uncle's good taste might be curious to visit the Secret City. The emperor is known to welcome visitors most kindly."

The earl beamed at her praise. "I will most certainly take that into consideration for the future."

"As will I," Reginald added with a purr.

Jili bowed and withdrew as the earl turned his attention to a group of barely clad women juggling sticks set on fire, and others carved to look like giant cocks.

Graham placed his hand on her back and led her toward a quieter spot. "Why did you ask the earl if he'd ever been to Eastshyre? What did you see?"

She frowned. "One of his rings. I thought the stone was familiar. A golden diamond...so rare, they are hardly ever allowed out of Eastshyre. But I could have been mistaken." Her gaze took in the rowdy scene. "Emperor Shiruto makes certain no man in the kingdom is wealthier than he is. He says it makes a man too ambitious and willing to betray. He taxes them unmercifully."

Graham snorted. "I suppose King Edgar should take Rulfert down a notch or two. But the earl practically paid for the war that let him regain his crown. Money does have its uses." He waved to a group of men off to the side, a lower class of knights than the ones seated near Rulfert. "'Tis a shame the earl has already declared his favorite...Bertram, of course. Makes the competition less than fair."

"So why do they come if they know they cannot win?" Jili picked her way along the edges of the crowd, Graham following close behind.

"There is more to a tournament than winning. Many knights have no land or money of their own. They are younger brothers, like me, or bastards whose fathers paid for their training and nothing more. They hope to make a decent enough showing to be hired by someone like the earl, or another of the lords who come to watch...fed and sheltered through the winter. Mayhaps scraping out a better life than that of toiling in the fields."

"So why are you here?" She turned and stared up at him, the evening light flickering across her face, casting exotic shadows on her skin.

She was smart, he realized. She saw things that most people didn't. She would be a valuable ally...or a deadly enemy. It aroused him to think of her power, imagining nights where they lay in bed, sweaty from sex and discussing the latest news of the court. To his surprise he found he liked the idea. Politics had always bored him before, but Jili gave them a whole new interest. His cock roused. She intrigued him no end.

"I am here to please my mothers." On impulse he reached out and tugged at a lock of her long black hair. "And the queen."

Her smile was enigmatic. "Ah."

"What the hell is that supposed to mean?" She obviously thought she was as clever as he did, the wench. He would have to make certain she never knew how much it impressed him. Nevertheless, he took her arm as they looked for a seat on one of the overly crowded tables.

The very next thing he saw was Bertram throwing amused glances their way. "Hellfire," Graham muttered, leading Jili as far away as possible.

She placed her hand on his arm. "Sit. I will take care of everything." When he shook his head, her eyes narrowed. "'Tis the proper way of things," she admonished, turning on her heel to make her way to where piles of food were being set out for the communal meal.

Not a single man in the entire square could keep his eyes off her as she moved gracefully across the ground, Graham saw with a grimace. Not that he blamed them. She was as fine as any highborn lady and as tough as any warrior. The combination made her irresistible. Graham's mood darkened as he acknowledged the fact, swearing he would break any man's arm who dared to touch her. His mood plummeted even further when Bertram rose and joined him.

"Just checking to see if you have quite recovered," the man said with a mocking smile. "I could send my *chirurgeon* to take a look at that arm."

"No thanks," Graham shot back with what he hoped was an amused expression. "I'd rather have Jili take care of my needs any day."

"And night." When Bertram laughed Graham clenched his fists. "I heard her screams. In fact, I believe the entire camp did. Tell me...is she for sale? I would be more than happy to—"

He got no further. Graham exploded across the table, grabbing the other man by the neck. The stitches in his arm popped open as he lifted the prince from his seat and pulled his face to his. "You will treat the lady with the respect she deserves," Graham bit out before throwing the man back down on the bench.

"Lady is it?" Bertram narrowed his eyes and gave Graham a calculating glare. "So that's how it is? You've fallen in love with the chit." He raised his glass in a bitter salute. "Then I wish you the best of it."

Hearing the sourness in the man's tone, Graham suddenly realized that so far, Bertram had not worn any woman's favor onto the field. Not once had he seen a scarf or ribbon tied to the prince's lance or armor.

Jili returned with ale, giving Bertram a respectful look. "Sir," she acknowledged before turning to Graham. "Should I bring another plate?"

He nodded. "And more to drink. Tell the serving girls to send out pitchers of the stuff." If he could get Bertram drunk enough he might learn something useful.

Although Jili frowned at the broken stitches, she refrained from comment. Graham tore a piece from his shirt and wrapped it around the wound. It would do for now. He took a long drink of ale and studied the prince.

"Have you no noble maiden whimpering for your hand in marriage?"

Bertram grimaced. "My mother has paraded several dozen or more for my inspection. And to a one, they have been the most boring, simple-minded creatures I have ever had the misfortune to meet."

Graham nodded in agreement. "And they look to snap like twigs in the marriage bed. Hell, I'd rather top a willing harlot than be forced to rut an ice-maid."

Bertram's shoulders slumped. "But at least you have a choice in the matter."

"True. My eldest brother, bless his bastard heart, has already produced a suitable heir. My mothers couldn't be happier. I'm completely off the hook." He smiled when he saw the other man's expression darken even more.

"'Twas my sorry lot to be the only son. The pressure, I tell you, is unbelievable. I have been forced to learn to play the harpsichord, take dance lessons, and wear shoes that would make a real man cry."

Graham chuckled, remembering the foppishly fashionable shoes at court. The damn things had such high heels and pointed toes they could make a torturer smile. He'd steadfastly refused to even contemplate them.

Bertram downed the last of his ale and leaned close. "And have you seen the latest clothes they are forcing men to wear?" He shuddered. "Breeches so tight they cut off all blood to the cock and leave your balls aching for days. I threatened to cut them down the middle and let my meat hang free. Now wouldn't that have been a magnificent sight?"

"Better yours than mine. I have enough trouble fighting off the women as it is."

"No doubt your squire will take care of that for you from now on." The prince's eyes narrowed suddenly, his mood changing in a second. "I know why you're here, Duncemore. Don't try and deny it," he added when Graham shook his head. "My mother and your mothers are thick as a band of thieves. You begin your training the same time I begin mine? Not a likely coincidence. Well, at least you earned the knighthood," he said with a grudging respect. "I don't know another man who could have kept my sister's carriage from crashing down that cliff." His expression had now lost any hint of its earlier geniality. "But if you interfere with my affairs in any way at all, I will have you thrown out of Westmyre."

Graham let his own expression harden. "I will do what I have been ordered to do, Your Highness," he answered. Despite any sympathy he might have for the man, Graham had a duty to the crown. And the ass was not yet in charge.

"Back out of the tournament," the prince ordered. "Go

home and get the hell out of my life. I don't need one of my mother's lapdogs nipping at my heels." He stood.

Graham rose also, and lowered his head in a gesture of respect. "Your Highness."

When Bertram snarled and stormed off, Graham smiled. He'd just found a new and fascinating way to torment the idiot prince.

"What was that all about?" Jili plopped three plates on the table and nodded to Bertram's empty seat. "How did you manage to piss him off so soon?"

Graham laughed, digging into the thick lamb chop and roasted onions with relish. "I called him 'your highness'. Do you believe it? I get to show my respect and make him furious all at the same time."

Jili, however didn't look so amused. "It would be better to have him as friend than enemy," she stated, nibbling at the plate of lettuce and vegetables she usually called a meal. "His station brings more than its share of separation."

Graham found himself staring at Bertram's untouched plate with less satisfaction than before. He hadn't seen his brothers for weeks, and spent less and less time with them now they were married with lives of their own. The prince had no other brothers—the reason the queen had been so adamant about him not participating in the tournament—and he was constantly surrounded by groveling toadies. What would his brothers do to him if he were in that situation?

His mood swung full circle as he saw the now obvious truth. Brothers were made for one of two things. Guarding your back when you needed it, and making damn certain you never took yourself too seriously.

His new buddy Bert was in for the time of his life. He finished his plate in a few large bites, and downed the other just as fast. "I've suddenly remembered something I left on the field," he said, giving Jili a fond smile. "I'll meet you back at the tent. I promise I won't be long." He winked, glared at all the other men watching, and made his way to the tilting yard, whistling a happy tune.

Old Bert needed a friend, Jili had said. Well, he would give the wanker all that and more.

The tilting dummy sat silent and alone as Graham made his way across the field. One or two squires were still at their labors, polishing armor and checking their masters' weaponry for the following day's events. They waved at him as he passed, and Graham waved serenely back. 'Twas a beautiful evening, he thought with a smile as he studied the tilting dummy. A beautiful evening that would turn into a beautiful night, and then into a beautiful day. He had just one or two adjustments to make, and everything would be ready for Bert on the morrow. He continued to whistle as he worked...enjoying each and every minute.

℘

He followed when she left the square, trailing her as she picked her way to the tent and slipped inside. She was distracted, unaware of his presence. Careless.

Although she might prove useful.

He thought of the days ahead. Everything would be carried out in its proper form and order. Even in this ignorant country where no one could appreciate his obedience to tradition, the ritual would be followed precisely.

In the shadow cast by the lantern in her tent, he watched as she stripped off her shirt and cleaned herself with a cloth and water. Beautiful, he admitted in detached admiration.

But beauty meant nothing...it was as fleeting as cherry blossoms in the spring.

Chapter Four

Snapdragon watched Rose come scurrying into the garden. "This can't be good," she muttered to Pansy, before pretending to be sound asleep.

Pansy barely twitched an eyebrow. After several glasses of sweet summer wine, she was as lazy as a slug.

The two fairies were sprawled on a wisteria vine climbing along the garden fence behind Finella and Samantha's manor house. It was just past supper, but the two had gotten an early start on the wine, and had barely managed to stay awake through the evening meal.

Rose had refused to join them...in fact she had been pensive all week, mumbling nonsense about how their newest charge was about to get into a whole lot of trouble.

Of course the boy was going to get into trouble. He was a Dunmore. But as far as Snapdragon and Pansy could tell, there was nothing that needed their immediate attention.

Rose, however thought differently. "Get up, the both of you," she ordered, standing beneath the thick-leaved plant with a stern look on her face. "We're going to the tournament."

"Of course we are, dear," Pansy soothed in her best Rose voice. "Next week with the rest of the family."

"Next week," Snapdragon echoed.

Rose's voice grew sterner when she spoke again. "If you do not come down this instant, I will go and find that ginger-striped cat. You know, the one who sharpens her claws every hour of the day, and who thinks you two are nothing more than a nice fat pair of rats."

Snapdragon's eyes flew open. "You wouldn't dare!"

"Care to bet?" Rose shrugged and turned to go. "Oh, well, don't say I didn't warn you. I'll be safely in the kitchen, should you change your mind." She turned and strode casually toward the gate.

Pansy sat up with a grimace. "Wait, Rose." She slid down the vine and Snapdragon followed, grumbling the entire time. "What do you think is so terrible it can't wait another few days?"

"There is great danger."

Snapdragon snorted. "There's no great danger. It's just a simple summer tournament." She rolled her eyes and Pansy chuckled.

Rose's expression darkened even more. "I can't explain it. I just know we have to get there...soon."

"Right." Pansy gave Snapdragon a conspiratorial wink. "There will be lots of lovely knights there. Lovely, sweaty, arms bulging—"

"Ooooo." Snapdragon was practically drooling as she turned her attention back to Rose. "Why didn't you say so in the first place? Let's go tell Finella and have her find someone to take us. How about that fabulous stablehand? I could ride on his shoulder any day."

Pansy nodded enthusiastically.

Rose shook her head just as hard. "Can't do that. The entire Dunmore clan is here, remember? The ladies need all the help they can get to make certain everyone else gets there on time. They are all so proud of Graham...and we can't interfere with family, remember?" She glanced pointedly at Pansy who had the decency to blush.

"Section sixty-five, sub-section three."

"Thank you, dear. Come along, now." Rose scurried toward the back of the garden and into the field beyond, leaving Snapdragon and Pansy to follow as best they could until they came to the edge of a tiny lake surrounded by a flock of beautiful white birds.

"Swans," Rose cooed in delight. "They should be big enough to carry us on their backs. Won't this be fun?"

Pansy gazed rapturously at the graceful birds. "Oh, Rose, what an excellent idea."

Even Snapdragon seemed impressed. "I have to admit, it does look like fun."

Rose skipped over to one and placed her hand on its neck. "This is Snowball. We've become great friends, haven't we?" The swan ducked its head and nuzzled her cheek.

Pansy giggled and ran to throw her arms around another bird's long white neck, with Snapdragon practically nipping at her heels. But Pansy slipped in a pile of swan droppings and screamed, crashing into her chosen bird who honked in startled indignation and flapped one wing, sending the fairy flying into another swan's rump.

When the huge bird jumped as if it had been shot, Snapdragon laughed so loud the entire flock of swans stood and looked for the danger. One ran headlong at Snapdragon, its wings flapping madly as it ducked its head and bit her on the nose. She retaliated by kicking it on the leg, and the bird snapped at her again, tearing a hunk of material from her dress.

In the meantime, Pansy had managed to crawl on another swan's back, only to have the bird arch its neck completely around, grab her arm and toss her into the lake. When Snapdragon laughed at her expense, Pansy wiggled her fingers and dragged the other fairy in beside her. Snapdragon cursed impressively and dunked Pansy underwater.

By now, all of the swans had taken to the air, except the one who watched in interest beside Rose.

"This is not exactly what I had planned," Rose said as she watched the watery battle. "I guess I should have known better," she added in resignation, as the fight showed no sign of stopping. "They're going to have a very cold ride," she finished with an evil smile. "A very, very cold ride."

☙

Jiliana's head shot up, the cloth held motionless in her hand as ripples of awareness prickled along her skin.

She was being watched.

When the tent-flap fluttered she blew out the candle and grabbed her shirt, shrugging it on with one hand while the other reached for her *katana*. Raising the blade high above her head, she waited in silence as one huge shoulder pushed its way into the tent.

"My, my, my," Graham said in appreciation, his gaze locking on the swath of skin that peeked from her unfastened shirt, despite the fact he couldn't see much in the dark. "Do I at least get to kiss you before you chop off my head?"

Jiliana lowered the blade, a worried frown still tugging at her brow. "Someone was watching." Her mood lifted as Graham's smile widened.

"All right, you caught me. I could see you silhouetted by the light, and could not tear my eyes away." He sat on the bed and crooked one finger. "Took me a few minutes to realize I was standing by my own tent, and the vision I saw was waiting inside for me." He held out his foot.

With a snort, Jiliana knelt and tugged off one big boot. "What took you so long?"

He laughed, the rumbling sound reminding her of a tiger's purr. "Were you so lonely without me?" He grabbed a handful of her hair and pulled her from the floor, dragging her on top of him as he lay back on the bed. "I was more than lonely without you." His other hand slid beneath the hem of her shirt, stroking the skin of her back as he touched his lips to hers.

The kiss was slow and deliberate. It started soft, a whisper of his lips against hers, but soon deepened into a demand, his mouth slanting over hers with a possessiveness that set her senses soaring. While she had read many of the great love poems of the east, she had never before understood the need to give oneself over completely to another...until Graham had come back into her life.

A tremble of nervousness fluttered in her stomach, quickly soothed by the rumble of want that sounded in Graham's throat. Hunger rose on swift wings between them, drawing them close in its shadowed embrace.

The knock on the tent-post took them both by surprise.

"This had better be important," Graham called out in a rough voice, moving his mouth to Jili's throat.

"Sir," came an equally gruff voice from outside. "Sir Bertram requests you attend him."

"Now? The fool's got to be joking." Graham's sigh of frustration was audible. "Tell him I have already gone to bed, and will attend him first thing in the morning."

"You better go see what he wants," Jiliana whispered in his ear, fighting against her own frustration. "What if something is wrong?"

"Something better damned well be very wrong." Graham brushed his lips against her hair as he rolled her over and reluctantly sat up. "Tell your master I will be with him shortly." He gave Jiliana a lingering look that made her want to beg him to stay. "I won't be gone long."

She smiled in understanding. "One must always put duty first."

"Whoever told you that was never in your bed," he answered, trailing his fingers across her stomach. "I am beginning to truly hate that man," Graham added, pulling his boot back on before ducking out the door.

Graham knew the minute he entered the prince's tent the night was not going to go well. Silk pillows and soft fur rugs were strewn over the floor, next to trays filled with wine and ale from every part of the kingdom. Mostly naked dancers writhed to a sultry drum-beat, descending on him like a swarm of locusts as soon as he'd been granted entrance.

And in the midst of all the decadence, Bert sat surrounded by half a dozen of the loveliest women there.

"Well, well, well." Graham bent over to step beneath a fall of silk draped from the ceiling. "To what do I owe this honor?" He smiled wolfishly at the woman dressed in only several long pearl necklaces who handed him a mug of ale. "My thanks."

Jili would be appalled at the obvious excess, he thought, sitting where the prince indicated. As his mind pictured her dressed in nothing but strands of jewels, his cock raised its head in anticipation. Decadent it might be, but he knew she would move even more gracefully than the dancers in the tent.

In fact, the more he studied them, the more they seemed to lack a certain...elegance. Whereas Jili moved with an effortless poise and style, these women were too practiced. Too vulgar, he realized in amazement as his mind finally grasped the truth. What would have set his loins on fire not so many weeks ago now looked base and pitiably put-on.

He took a long drink and studied Bert over the rim of the glass. What did the princeling have planned for him tonight?

"Beautiful, aren't they?" The prince pulled one of his harem close and pinched a heavily rouged nipple. The color smeared, and for the very first time in his life, Graham was actually embarrassed to be in such debauched and wanton company.

"You would pay for nothing but the best," he answered smoothly before finishing his ale and motioning for another. "Surely you didn't bring them all with you? 'Twould not seem right that a lowly knight could afford such expensive entertainment."

"A gift from Earl Rulfert to his favorite in the tournament. He sends them from the castle every night." Bert laughed and nudged his hand between the woman's legs. She gasped in a contrived voice and licked her lips at Graham.

He smiled back, not enjoying the show in the least. "The earl knows who you are." On some level Graham had known it all along.

"Of course."

"How many others? Your anonymity grows weaker by the day."

The prince shrugged one shoulder negligently. "As long as the men continue to challenge me in the lists, I don't care who knows." He dismissed the subject in the blink of an eye, his smile growing feral in the flickering light of the candles. "I have a challenge for you." A motion of his hand had six women flocking to sit with Graham, a perfect match for the prince's companions.

Graham raised a mocking brow. "A challenge you will undoubtedly fail." He drank the second glass faster than the first and gestured for a third.

Bert laughed and the women added their chorus of vapid giggles. Graham made a pretense of stroking the hair of the woman who'd put her head on his lap. She smelled of liquor and stale sex, a combination that his treacherous manhood refused to be aroused by.

When her hand inched slowly toward his crotch, he grabbed the woman's wrist and growled. She laughed, but did not move to touch him again. Bert's eyes narrowed in dark amusement and Graham knew that he'd seen the gesture for what it truly was...a revulsion he couldn't hide.

"I heard you topped five women in a single night," Bert said carelessly. "A record we both share."

Graham snorted.

The prince continued without a pause, glancing pointedly at the dozen women between them. "Six each. I'll wager I finish mine long before you finish yours." He spread his legs and pulled one woman's head between his thighs, rubbing his groin into her face. Her fingers caressed him through his breeches as her teeth worked to untie the lacings. The prince gritted his teeth as she stroked him into full arousal.

"I assume you are offering a prize." Graham reached across one of his harlots to snag a honeyed fig from a tray. He wondered what Jili's skin would taste like smeared with the sweet fruit. He vowed to find out the soonest chance he got.

The girl had managed to untie the prince's breeches and now tugged them down with her teeth. When his manhood sprang free, she sucked it hard into her mouth. Bert groaned, but still sipped casually at his wine.

"What do you want, Duncemore? I have it in my power to give you your own estate...make you a lord, not just the youngest bastard son."

A second woman joined the first, the two now taking turns milking Bert with their mouths. The prince's hips jerked up to meet them, his cock a thick and turgid purple. And Graham was not completely immune to the erotic scene being played out before him, his thoughts time and again picturing Jili kneeling between his thighs, the tight heat of her mouth sucking him to perfect completion.

Graham bit back his groan of frustration as Bertram growled, tangled his hands in one woman's hair and held her hard against him as he thrust deeper and deeper into her mouth until he finally came with a roar of elation.

Clenching his teeth against the surge of need that pounded into his own rousing cock, Graham fought back his hunger in uncharacteristic denial.

The prince sat back with a sigh and smiled at the two licking his still swollen length. "That was excellent, my dears," he praised, with a brilliant smile to both of them. To his credit, Bert treated his trollops well. Graham had seen many men of high station use these women with a meanness that was completely uncalled for.

"One for me," the prince stated with a satisfied smile. "Your turn."

Two of the women seated by Graham knelt and spread his legs apart, but he shook his head and shooed them away. "I do not care to be a lord. Llewellyn has more than earned his title."

"Ah." Bert studied Graham intently. "Then perhaps I have some other prize that I could tempt you with. Come, Lila." At his imperial command, another woman came to plant herself on the prince's lap. She was much younger than the others, and extraordinarily pretty.

When Bert tucked his hand between her legs, she slid her knees apart, her eyes closing in utter delight as his fingers stroked hard over the nub of her clit. She laid her head against his chest as her legs shook and her hips began to buck against his hand. But the prince was overly careful not to dip into her at all, pulling back each time she arched her body to urge him to touch her further.

"Have your attention now?" Bert's face was as sharp as a hawk's. "Beautiful, isn't she. And never been penetrated...not even by my own hand. Would you like to see?"

At his nod, the girl bent her knees and let them fall completely apart, giving Graham a firsthand view of the bait dangled before him. The prince reached out and spread her lips even more, opening her tiny pink cunt for Graham's closer inspection.

"A pretty piece, I'll grant you that." Graham's flesh stirred anew as the prince continued to strum the swollen pearl of her clit and her cries of pleasure echoed around them.

"Completely untried, and yet willing and ready to come at your command. Shall I make her come for you now, Duncemore? Would you care to see how that tight little cunt would clamp around a man, hear how she would scream when you impaled her on your cock?"

Graham took another long drink of ale and casually motioned for another, more intrigued by this proposition than he should have been. On another day he would have taken the girl without hesitation, doing whatever the other man demanded to be the first to pluck so juicy a cherry.

Bertram grinned in feral delight as he noticed Graham's hesitation. He stopped his play between Lila's legs and she whimpered in sudden distress. "Or should I send her away to spend the night wanting?"

Graham did not like this new turn of events. "Wherever did you find her?" he asked instead, still unable to tear his gaze away.

Bert stroked her slowly once more. "She is actually the daughter of a very good friend...a rather lustful duchess who did not want to raise a bastard child. Her bloodline is royal—on both sides, and while her family will never claim her, I will publicly vouch for her lineage. She would make an excellent wife, in more ways than one."

The girl's breath came out in short hot pants, and Graham felt sweat break out along his brow. Damn, but she was beautiful in her passion, her cunt darkening to a deep rose pink as it opened and thickened as if demanding to be breached.

The prince fingered the wet that dripped from her sex, smearing the juice down and around the even tinier pucker of her ass. He fingered the ring of muscle and the girl screamed in frustration, wiggling desperately against his touch as if trying to force him to give her more. Very gently, Bert tapped against this other opening, his smile growing darker with every passing minute.

Graham fought down his own need as he watched Bert tease the small pink hole.

"Did I mention she has already shown a great interest in other forbidden pleasures?" He slicked more juice between her cheeks. "Roll over on your hands and knees," he ordered, and Lila readily complied, arching her bottom high into the air with her head laid down on her arms. Graham could see her every muscle jerk in anticipation as Bert took the tip of his pinky and gently eased it into the quivering circle of her ass.

Lila screamed again, more desperate this time as the prince

eased his finger in and out, never breaching her more than a fraction of an inch.

Damn him to the worst of all possible hells, Graham cursed to himself as a new image implanted itself into his head. Jili on her hands and knees begging him to finger her ass.

"Care to try?" The prince smiled in delight at Graham as the girl wiggled and shook before him.

"What would you want in return?" Despite his best effort, Graham's voice was thick with need. He downed another glass of ale, hoping the drink might dull the edge of his spiraling arousal until he could escape to his own tent and ease himself in Jili's touch. He kept his hand clenched so tight around the cup he thought he might actually break it, but made no move to touch the girl.

"Your squire. She intrigues me. Not only beautiful, but deadly. And she would be a far more interesting bodyguard than the ogres my parents have forced upon me."

Graham choked on his mouthful of ale. "Not a chance."

"That is too bad." Bertram shrugged and went back to his sport, calling for one of the other women to assume Lila's same position before him. "Why don't we share a woman? I will give you first pick of whatever entrance most amuses you."

"What about the girl? Surely you don't intend to leave her in such agony."

The prince signed. "If you won't give me your squire, you can still have her for the night. Just swear to leave the tournament tomorrow and stay the hell out of my life."

Graham laughed, for the very first time appreciating the prince's gambit. The man knew how to strike a bargain, there was no doubt about it. Probably a very good trait to have as the future king.

"My duty is, and always will be, to my king," Graham said deliberately. "I have pledged my life to that service, and will never break the oath I have taken."

The prince frowned. "You could make quite an enemy here tonight," he added just as seriously. "Hope your enthusiasm doesn't come back to haunt you." He rose to his knees behind the woman and slid his breeches down his hips. "Go, Lila, take care of yourself," he ordered before spitting on his hand and slicking it in the crease of the woman's ass. He smacked her thigh when she whimpered, her eyes already closed in bliss. He smacked her hard again when she shuddered, his lips turning up sardonically. "I pay her well to feed my dark side." He twisted his hand in her hair and forced her head back. "If you do not care to join me in my pleasure, you will stay until I give you leave to go. My other guards have the entire night off."

It was an order, and both men knew it. Graham couldn't refuse. In complete and utter fury, he threw the glass of ale into the corner. If he was to guard the bastard prince, he couldn't afford to get drunk on the job. He stood and moved to stand at the doorway, doing his best to ignore the high-pitched screams as Bert slid the length of his cock hard and deep into the harlot's ass.

Chapter Five

Graham was as pissed off as he'd ever been by the time Bert released him for the day. He'd had no sleep at all for two nights running. His cock throbbed from the torture of having no release all night, and he couldn't get his mind off images of Jili in positions that would have made even his brothers blush.

She met him as he stormed into the tent, her face falling in sudden disappointment. "You smell like a whore," she accused, wrinkling her nose in disgust. "Is this how you spent the night?" She turned away, busying herself with his armor. "Not that it's any of my business."

Despite her flippant words, Graham could hear the note of betrayal in her voice. Bugger it all to hell! His guilt made him defensive, his frustration only adding to the fire. "'Tis none of your business," he snapped too hastily. "If I had wanted your opinion on the matter, I would have given it to you." Striding to where she had laid out a bowl of water and cloth, Graham dumped the entire thing over his head, the shock of the cold doing nothing to ease the discomfort of his body and mind.

Jili pressed her lips together and smoothed her face into a porcelain mask of composure. "I will have the boys bring food to break your fast, Sir Graham," she said stiffly, giving him a practiced bow.

Graham should have let her go in peace, or at the very least swallowed down his pride and told her what had really happened. He knew that...he really did. But what he found himself doing was another thing entirely—in fact, he could readily say it was one of the stupidest things he had ever done in his life.

Before she had a chance to make it out the door, he grabbed her wrist and spun her towards him, guiding her hand to his crotch. Just a couple of strokes was all it would take to ease the unbearable pain and calm him enough to face the day.

She'd already proven a willing student, this would be just another lesson, he reasoned, and a quick one at that. And tonight, he would make her come until she begged him to stop.

What woman would say no to such a fair and equitable trade? He gave her his best sheepish look—the one that had never failed him in the past—as he rubbed her hand along his turgid length.

"Please, Jili. I thought of you all night. I need you so mu— AHHHHH, SHITE," he bellowed when with the merest flick of her fingers, she twisted his wrist and bent it back upon itself, the simple movement causing an agony so great Graham fell to his knees on the ground before her, biting his tongue in the effort it took from pleading with her to release him.

"Spinal lock," she stated casually, glaring in satisfaction at the shock on his face. "Amazingly effective. So is this," she added keeping her fingers clamped around his wrist as she took a step toward the door.

Graham grunted in pain, having no choice but to follow her like a dog follows its master. After long and dangerous seconds of silently vowing to wring her lovely little neck, Graham took a good hard look at his situation and decided he wasn't in as dire a predicament as he'd first believed. Her perfectly shaped ass was just inches from his face, and when she turned to glare down at him again, he took full advantage. Wrapping his other arm around her waist, he pulled her close and pressed his lips to her stomach, wedging his head between her breasts.

He felt her tremble even as the pressure on his wrist increased. He groaned in pain, making damned certain she could feel his breath on the peak of skin peeping out beneath her shirt.

At long last, his reason returned...or so he thought until he heard the next words that came tumbling from his throat. "I swear to you, I did not so much as touch another woman last night, despite the throngs of whores the prince paraded for my pleasure. The best I've ever seen," he added, digging his grave even deeper. "And he had this one girl, Lila, who had the most perfectly shaped cun—Damn it, Jili, that really hurts," he finished when she snapped his jaw shut with her knee. The force of it knocked his teeth together so hard his ears started ringing. "What was that for?"

"Being the biggest ass I have ever had the sorry chance to meet."

"I was trying to explain, woman, that I haven't done anything wrong."

"Save it," she retorted, finally releasing his wrist, "for someone who might actually give a shite."

And with that, she flew out into the morning, leaving him cursing and confused, wondering exactly what he'd done to deserve such unjust treatment.

The bright rays of the rising sun did little to lift Jiliana's mood. She had acted like a jealous lover when Graham came back this morning. And even though she knew he must be beyond weary, she had accused him of spending the night whoring without bothering to listen to his explanation.

Not that he had one. She felt her jealousy sharpen its claws again as she remembered his description of the beautiful virgin the prince had displayed for his taking.

Assuming the first position of the *kata,* she tried to focus on the movements. She was becoming far too attached to her handsome master. What had she been thinking when she'd asked him to take her to bed? And that was exactly what she wanted, she admitted, stubbing her toe as she shifted her balance and dropped low to the ground in the next position.

Stupid mistake, she berated herself, trying to force her thoughts back to the task at hand.

And, in truth, the only thing Graham had promised was that he would never hurt her. Unless she let him. She knew her body was safe in his arms, he'd proven that already. Her heart, however, was a completely different matter, and she hadn't taken its betrayal into consideration.

How could she have made such an error in judgment? *The only person one can ever hope to know is oneself, and in the knowing, one can achieve enlightenment.* Jiliana had misjudged her feelings for Graham. She had paid them less attention than she should have.

She froze as she turned to see him walking toward her, his huge shadow falling to block out the sunlight.

"I'm sorry," he said, his eyes dark and solemn. "I promised I would never force you."

She shook her head too fast in denial. "You didn't." He copied as she moved into the next part of the form, both arms crossing over the chest before one fist shot out in a strike while the other fist pulled back to settle against the hip. "I should have believed you. You've never lied to me before...have you?"

He rubbed his wrist and gave her a wounded smile. When he held up his pinky, Jili's heart beat faster. "And I never will.

Deal?"

"Deal."

They finished the *kata* in silence.

"I have a surprise planned for old Bert today." Graham bought a sausage on a stick from one of the camp vendors as they made their way to the tilting yard. His smile grew overly sunny.

"Oh?" Jiliana munched an apple and a handful of nuts. "Do I really want to know?"

"Hell yes! After what he put us both through last night, he's owed every bit of this today. Watch a true master at work," he added, lifting her easily over the fence.

"Uh huh." Jiliana tried not to frown. When Graham seemed that pleased with himself, disaster was sure to follow.

The prince strode onto the field early as he always did. Jiliana watched warily as Graham walked over to meet him. "Good morrow, Bert," he called, and she had to grin when she saw the annoyance that crossed the prince's face.

"Duncemore," came the terse reply. "You are out early."

"'Tis the early bird that catches the worm." Graham winked. He scratched his chest and stretched as if he'd just woken up from a good night's sleep instead of being two long days without it. "Shall we warm up? I took the liberty of having your horse saddled and ready."

The prince's gaze moved from Graham to Jiliana and back again. But Graham's face held not a trace of guile, and her innocence was honest—she hadn't a clue what he was up to.

"Very well," Bertram finally answered. "You have the tilting dummy ready?"

Graham nodded enthusiastically. "Yes, sir...you ass," he mouthed to Jiliana as the prince turned to mount his steed.

Now she knew he was up to something. "*Graham.*" Her whisper was cut short when the prince motioned for his lance.

He was dressed in only the heavily quilted gambeson this morning, full armor being too hot and heavy for practice. He wore thick leather gauntlets as opposed to metal, and had forsworn a helmet. Everyone knew Sir Bertram excelled at the tilting dummy. Because he never missed, he was lax about wearing any decently protective gear.

Graham handed him the lance with a grin. "Would you like to wait for a wee bit longer? There are so few ladies here to admire your strength of form."

When the prince snorted, Jiliana ducked her head to keep him from seeing her amusement. He was as big a braggart as Graham, the two of them liking nothing better than to go head to head when a decent crowd had gathered to watch.

"Or I could go first?" Graham added in earnest. It was also a bone of contention that Graham was every bit as good as the prince in the joust. After the very first day of practice, the prince had told Graham in no uncertain terms that he was always to be the first in line...and that the knight was forbidden to practice until the prince had already left the field.

An arrogant shake of Sir Bertram's head gave his answer.

"As you wish," Graham added, stepping calmly away.

They watched as the prince circled the field several times, calling orders to his squires in a sharp and commanding voice, pretending not to waste time as he waited for the crowd to gather.

Graham's face grew more smug by the minute.

"What did you do?" Jiliana demanded, glaring up at him.

He puckered his lips and blew out a few cheery notes. "A little trick my older brothers showed me many years ago. And since Bert doesn't have any older brothers, this should come as a great surprise. Oh, look. He's almost ready to go."

The prince sat stiff and proud atop his horse as he readied for his first pass. Graham's smile grew dark. "Hold 'er steady," he yelled as the horse took off at a gallop.

Other knights and squires, hearing the commotion, came to watch.

The prince's lance was aimed perfectly as he and his mount approached the target. A solid hit would cause the dummy to swing around the poll in an arc. If the knight-in-training did not follow through, the dummy's back arm—which was weighted with sand—would complete the circle and knock him off his horse. Only a well-skilled marksman could hit the target arm hard enough to swing the dummy full around and gallop out of range in time to escape further damage.

"What did you do?" she demanded once more as the prince's lance struck home.

The dummy arm swung out...stopped...and swung back again to catch the prince full in the chest, sending him flying from his horse to land in an ignoble heap on the ground.

The gathered crowd roared in laughter as Bertram let loose a string of curses, his temper flaring out of control.

"Dumbass...he needs to learn a sense of humor. His men expect it," Graham muttered beneath his breath before he laughed the loudest and moved to help the other man to his feet. "My mistake, my friend," he guffawed. "I completely forgot to take off the safety catch. Guess I didn't get enough sleep last night. Are you well?"

"Serves the boy right," someone muttered behind her. "Too big fer 'is breeches."

It was something she had heard more and more often over the past couple of days. Sir Bertram, it seemed, was acting far above his station, treating his fellow knights as if they were nothing more than servants meant to do his bidding. Young, brash, and spoiled, the prince was not making friends among his supposed peers. While his natural air of command sent most other knights doing his bidding without thinking, they did not actually like the man.

Too bad, Jiliana thought. It was a rare chance a future king got to mingle among his people. The prince was assuredly not making the most of his unique opportunity. His face was flushed in anger as Graham followed him from the field. The other knights made no secret of their continued laughter at his expense.

Graham was the hero in their eyes. He was as well loved as the prince was not. They were perfect examples of the two opposing principles taught by the masters of the east. Only by an integration of the two could one ever hope to achieve balance.

She saw him pull the prince aside, talking to him in a serious tone. Occasionally the other man's head would lift and he would glance around, the anger receding from his expression as a sharp intellect took its place.

When the two finally parted ways, Graham was nodding his head in satisfaction as he watched the prince plaster on a smile and take the ribbing much more jovially.

Graham had to wait his turn as several more knights took the field after the dummy was working correctly once more. He leaned cheerfully against the fence, watching each man's technique and bellowing out encouragement.

The prince had vanished after the second knight mounted, and Jiliana wondered where he'd gone. He usually stayed to watch with the rest, learning each knight's weaknesses and strengths. A rustling in the grass caused her to look down to see Bertram crawling over the ground with a long rope in his hands.

He grinned up at her and placed his finger to his lips, his face so excited Jiliana kept her silence. She'd seen these rituals time and again at the school in Kyomo, and they never failed to fascinate her.

Only her eyes moved as she watched the prince slip the rope through the fence, around both of Graham's feet, and back through the fence on the other side. After tying it decently tight around the post, the prince crawled several feet away before he stood and walked toward Graham with a smile.

"Care to spar? I have a match with Sir Herbert this afternoon and could use a bit of loosening up...that is, if you're not too tired."

As expected, Graham took the bait. "Tired? Not after missing just two nights' sleep. Jili, hand me my swo—" He took a single step and fell flat on his face as the rope tangled his feet together.

The prince laughed in complete abandon, the assembled knights and squires adding their hoots of amusement. Even Jiliana choked on a giggle when she saw Graham's shocked expression.

"Why you—" He jumped to his feet in a flurry of movement, but the prince was faster. He'd already made it half-way across the field before Graham began the chase.

"Who ya bettin' on darling," called an aging squire to Jiliana's right. "Sir Graham may be big, but Sir Bertram's got a good 'ead start."

"I think I'll save my coin," she said with a grin. "Depending on the outcome, I could be out of a job by noon."

She shook her head and headed toward the stables, the sounds of laughter following behind. Graham and Sir Bertram might be at their game for hours, but it was a good thing. She had seen many a friendship mature from an initially heated competition.

The stable was quiet when she slipped inside to check on Graham's horse. The great beast grazed regally in his stall, as if he knew how beautiful he was. Like horse, like master. Jiliana smiled ruefully, tossing the steed an apple.

A wisp of shadow flicked over the edge of her vision, gone before she could catch it, but it caused her gut to clench. Her hand on the hilt of her *katana*, she moved deeper into the stable, past other stalls and stacks of hay until she reached the very back of the building. There, half-buried in straw, lay a figure shaking and gasping for breath.

Jiliana rushed to kneel by the boy whose face was contorted in agony as the spasms continued to rack his body. Blood-flecked foam spewed from his lips as his eyes sought hers in silent supplication. He tried to speak, but his jaw was locked, the poison already paralyzing his muscles. She could do nothing but watch in horror as his life ebbed slowly and painfully away. When she was certain he was gone, her fingers strayed to brush a fall of hair from his face. He couldn't have seen more than fifteen summers, she thought as the rush of sorrow overtook her.

Far too young to have met his death—as so many others. Could she not escape her sins even here?

With a sigh, she closed his eyes and began to examine the rest of his body. She knew he had been poisoned, but who had done it and why? Then she saw that the boy bore Bertram's emblem on the sleeve of his tunic.

Two men dead in three days who both labored for the prince? Not a likely coincidence. Jiliana began a closer inspection. She pried open his mouth to look for a piece of food he might have eaten before turning the boy's head to search for an entry wound. Nothing. And nothing on his chest, either. She pulled a knife from her belt and had just begun to cut off his tunic when a loud voice yelled from behind.

"What have ye done?"

She turned to see a surly faced knight staring at her in repulsion. Sir Herbert, she recalled, a man known for his nearly fanatical loyalty to the crown. This was not going to work in her favor. "Sir Herbert, I found the boy already dying. I was trying to find out what had killed him and how." She kept her own voice calm and even.

The knight stepped closer and inspected the body just as she had done. "'Tis one of Sir Bertram's men." He came quickly to the same conclusion that she had. "Two men of the same house lost in a few days. This smells of a deliberate act." He frowned. "Aren't ye the one who was so certain no animal had killed the first man?" His tone grew suspicious. "And here ye are by the body of the second."

He drew his sword. "Move away," he ordered, "and keep your hands away from that foreign blade."

"Please." Jiliana stood slowly, holding her hands in full view between them, although she could have had her *katana* out and ready before the man could even see the movement. "Please call Sir Graham and Sir Bertram. I swear to you I am not involved in either of these deaths."

He snorted, but seemed relieved when she asked for the other knights to be present. Just then, several men came walking into the stable, stopping short in surprise when they saw the knight's blade leveled at her throat.

The sound of metal grating on metal filled the air as more swords were drawn.

"Sir Herbert," called an older knight. "The woman belongs

to Sir Graham. Best to leave her alone and find your pleasure elsewhere."

Herbert's face flushed an ugly red. "Bring Graham and Bertram. Another of Bertram's men is dead."

While the knights in question were being summoned, the rest of the men gathered close to Jiliana. *Too close.* She fought against her growing fear as memories rose to haunt her. The stench of smoke. The sounds of screaming. Her fingers itched to draw the *katana*, do something in defense as they crowded around her, the stench of their sweat and her growing dread triggering a cold and bleak emotion, one she knew too well. Dangerous. Deadly.

Until an old squire knelt and made his own appraisal. "Snakebite," he said, holding the boy's arm out for inspection. Two puncture wounds bit into the skin. "Doesn't happen often, but 'tis not unheard of. Leave the girl be, she's had no part in this."

One by one, the men sheathed their swords, still not moving far enough away for Jiliana's comfort. Only when Graham and Bertram arrived with furious looks on their faces did they step away and give her any room to breathe.

"What's happened?" The prince shoved men out of his way in his haste to reach the body. His face softened as he stared at the dead boy. Despite his arrogance, he was known as a fair and generous master, and Jiliana felt another wave of sorrow hit her when she saw the loss in his eyes.

"Snakebite," stated the squire once more. "An accident...nothing to do with Sir Graham's woman."

Although Bertram nodded and the knights dispersed, Jiliana remained unconvinced. Two deaths by two different animals in nearly as many days? Again, something oddly familiar tickled at her consciousness, and she was left with the disturbing feeling that she was missing something of great importance.

"What is it?" Graham demanded as they walked in silence back to their tent, his fingers wrapping around a stray lock of hair, the intimate gesture pulling her out of her musings. "Something wrong? You're not still mad at me?"

His expression was so woebegone she could barely suppress her smile. "You are too irresistible for your own good...or mine."

"I have a few hours until I am due at Bert's...we could sneak in a quick lesson." When he waggled his eyebrows her smile shown in earnest.

"You should get some sleep," she admonished, although she could already feel the tingle between her legs.

"Sleep?" He snorted. "A knight doesn't need no bloody stinkin' sleep."

Chapter Six

"'Tis your turn today." Graham nodded pointedly at the tub. "I get to watch."

Jiliana whirled to face him, her mood changing like a storm on the horizon. "You're not serious." She paced around the tub, keeping a lot of space between them. Surely he didn't...could not mean...to watch.

As his cock stiffened and his smile widened, she knew for certain he intended just that.

She grew less than amused as she eyed the steaming water. "I don't suppose you'd turn around while I undressed?" A stupid shyness overtook her as she traced every perfect line of his frame. She couldn't come close to matching his beauty.

"Not even the tiniest sliver of a chance." He sat on the bed and crossed his arms over his chest. "Unless you do not wish to continue our lessons. Which would be a terrible shame...you were doing so excellently well." If anything, he watched her more closely than before.

Jiliana found herself stepping farther from the tub. "Graham, I am not...I mean, if you expect—*kuso*," she finished, moving around the tub to stand directly before him. He would have to see sometime, and it would be better to know right from the start if he found her unusual look repulsive. "There were some things I never told you," she added in a very quiet voice, wishing again that she was not so different from other women, that she was perfect and unspoiled and—

In a sudden burst of anger, she fumbled at her shirt, unhooking the beautifully knotted fastenings. She couldn't change who she was, or what had happened. If he couldn't accept it, then he couldn't, and all the wanting in the world wouldn't be able to change his mind.

Nevertheless, she dropped her gaze as she shrugged the shirt from her shoulders, exposing a row of scars that ran over her shoulder and down toward her breast. She waited as calmly as she could for his gasp of revulsion, before braving a glance at him through her lashes.

Graham's eyes never wavered from her skin as he followed the pattern of the marks with his fingers. Now outlined by swirls of black ink, Jiliana fervently hoped the scar's harsh lines were softened by the design she'd had tattooed into her skin to mask the horrid wound.

"Show me more." Graham's voice had gone strangely thick and gentle.

Emboldened by his intrigue, she let her shirt fall completely open, exposing the design in its entirety. The stem of the rose twisted up her stomach, its leaves curling delicately around her breast and the flower opening over her shoulder. The scars had been hidden in the petals of the rose, and the burns on her stomach were covered by the gently curving stem.

"Tell me." He reached out and pulled her to him, splaying his palm across her stomach as his gaze rose to capture hers.

Jiliana trembled, this intimacy far beyond her expectations. A part of her wanted to escape his stare, curl back upon herself, alone and safe. But another part of her—a new and bolder woman—ordered her to stay...meet his intensity in equal measure. Her thoughts turned back to that fateful night so many years before.

"They burned the house."

He nodded in silent acknowledgement.

"They tied my father to the chair and made him watch while they—" She took a deep breath when he did not pull away. "After, they set the roof on fire. I could hear my father yelling, screaming at me to get up...but I hurt so much I could barely move. The first beam fell between us, cutting him off from the door—and he was still screaming, yelling at me to move, and I couldn't reach him, I couldn't find my way. When the second beam fell and landed on my shoulder, I heard him yell my name again. And I finally managed to crawl my way to the door, beneath the smoke..." Her voice trailed off of its own accord as memories she hadn't set free in years rose up to close her throat. "But I looked back. Once. Before the whole thing caved in...and I could see him, Graham. He was still there, alive, and the look on his face was so horrible, I will never forget it. Such blame and guilt and anger."

"And you think he was blaming you?" Graham's brows turned down. "That's the stupidest thing I've ever heard."

Jiliana felt her own anger rise at the carelessness of his words. "Thanks so much for your understanding." She snarled the sentence, shrugging her shirt back over her shoulders. She knew Graham could be an ass, but this was beyond nasty, even for him.

He chuckled when she stiffened and glared at him in furious silence. "You make the same mistake now that you made then." Both his hands curled around her waist and dragged her against him until she was standing between his thighs, hip to hip, their faces so close she could feel his breath against her neck. "What you saw was his anger at himself, Jili. That he could not protect you...that you might die along with him and there was nothing he could do to save you. He never blamed you...he blamed himself." He laid his head upon her shoulder and sighed. "It was how my father felt after my mother died."

Jiliana felt her confusion grow. "But I thought—Finella...Samantha?" She let her hands caress the back of his neck and threaded her fingers through his thick spiky hair.

"Finella and Samantha never once in my life treated me any differently than their own sons, and I adore them both—miserable meddlers that they are...but my mother died just after I was born. My father rarely spoke of her. I only know her name. Not where she was born, or who she called family." He pulled back and gave her a smile, nothing more than a twist of his lips. "Llewellyn is first born and Lord Dunmore. Hell, even my brother Allard has straightened up and become a judge. I thought that winning this tournament would prove that I was worthy of something—" He broke off and closed his eyes as if disgusted with his thoughts.

"Honor rises differently than pride, Graham." She rubbed the frown from his forehead. "Do not let your pride stand in the way of theirs."

He tugged at the sash tied around her waist, his eyes taking on a wicked glint. "Enough of all this maudlin talk. Does that gorgeous flower go any farther down?"

Jiliana felt her cheeks go warm. "Do you really like it?"

In answer, he picked her up and carried her to the tub, dropping her in clothes and all. "I will like it much better clean and sweet-smelling."

She spit water from her mouth and cursed him to hells she knew he'd never heard of, vowing to introduce him to each and every one as soon as she could possibly manage it, stopping only when he knelt down and took her mouth with his.

Desire arced between them as Graham thrust his tongue between her lips, the gesture sudden and demanding. A growing and familiar need spiraled from her stomach, the ache between her legs already begging for his touch.

He pulled away as quickly as he'd taken control, sitting back on his heels to gaze at her through eyes the color of the sky near night. "Take off your clothes," he ordered, no trace of teasing on his face. "I will not ask you again."

Jiliana bit her lip, not in confusion as she had done before, but with a rising wantonness that surprised her with its strength. "Am I beautiful?" she found herself asking as she sat up straight and let the shirt slide off her shoulders once again. She'd never cared to be beautiful in the past...beauty brought pain and fear and anger...but now, held tight in the safety of Graham's gaze, she wanted desperately to hear the words.

When he refused to say anything, she threw the shirt at his chest and stood, slowly untying the sash around her waist. "Tell me," she said, this time her voice catching on the words as some of her earlier doubt resurfaced.

In answer, he reached out and ran his hand up the inside of her thigh. "I have called many women beautiful. And at the time, I believed each of them were." He raised his face to meet hers, still kneeling on the floor beside her. "But you are beyond any woman I have met. To say you are beautiful doesn't do you justice." His eyes devoured her. "Exquisite...precious...rare— these are words that fit you better." He gave a pull and her *hakama* fell into the water around her feet, exposing her fully to his gaze. "Damn, woman, I swear I am speechless."

"That would be a first," she replied, sinking down into the water. But she had heard the truth in his voice, despite his attempt at flippancy. It was enough. It was more than enough.

She closed her eyes, enjoying the hot and steamy water. In

Eastshyre she had bathed frequently...trying to wash away the layers of her guilt. But since her return to Westmyre, she had reverted back to less stringent habits. She hadn't had a bath in weeks, other than to clean those parts necessary with a cloth at the end of the day. Now she wanted nothing more than to soak the cares of the day away—but Graham had already made other plans.

"Are you going stay in there all afternoon?" Jiliana winked one eye open to find him nodding his head at the bed. "I don't have a whole lot of time here."

"I didn't rush you," she complained.

"You're at least not going to wash your hair?" It was hard to keep from laughing at the whining tone of his voice.

"I hoped you might do that for me." She found the sodden cloth in the water and threw it at him without bothering to look. To her satisfaction, she heard the slap as it hit skin, and she chuckled in delight when he snorted his surprise.

"I would be happy to wash your hair."

She should have known by the way he agreed too readily that the man was up to something, but she jumped in shock when she felt him slip the cloth between her legs.

"You asked for it," he whispered in her ear as he rubbed the coarse material over her mound, dipping between the folds of her flesh to rub the sensitive spots between. Jiliana whimpered as the fire rose, parting her legs to allow him a greater freedom of movement. He moved the cloth to the tender pearl of flesh he had touched before, and she held her breath as the sensation shuddered through her. Already her thighs trembled in anticipation and her breath grew short and choppy.

Graham's chuckle rumbled against her neck. "Not yet, my warrior queen," he admonished, drawing his hand away. "We have too many things to explore first."

He filled one of the wooden buckets and dumped the water over her head. As Jiliana spluttered, vowing to knock him on his giant ass, he lowered his head and took one of her nipples in his mouth, the blissful gesture shocking her to silence. She arched against him, her arms curling around his head, pulling him closer as the cry of pleasure tumbled from her lips. "*Baka,*" she whispered, the endearment sipping easily from her tongue.

"What does that mean?" Graham pulled away, giving her a decently convincing frown.

"It means fool." She grinned when he nodded as if he'd known it all along before standing to move to the bed.

"Like I said before...are you going to stay in there all day?" He lay down and crossed his arms behind his head, giving her a perfect view of his toned chest and the impressive lump of his cock as it jutted towards his stomach. He whistled in feigned nonchalance and she felt her mood grow bright as the afternoon sun.

He made her smile...he made her laugh. Feel a joy she'd forgotten in her years of service and exile. And he made her body sing with a passion she'd never dreamed existed. The thought of what was to come slithered across her skin. In a burst of frenzied energy, Jiliana soaped and rinsed her hair— along with every other part of her she could reach, and leapt from the tub, soaking wet, to launch herself upon his chest.

His breath came out with a whoosh, but his arms curled around her like the sturdy roots of a tree, and he held her warm against his body, not muttering a single word of protest as she rained water down upon him.

"Happy now?" he demanded, spitting a sodden tendril of hair from his mouth. "Did you think I smelled as bad as all that? I did bathe a couple of days ago." Before she could even squeal, he rolled her over and pinned her beneath him, scratching his day old beard against her neck.

Jiliana's skin prickled all the way to her toes. "Graham, stop!" she ordered when he replaced his chin with his tongue, licking up the side of her face like a huge tiger grooming his mate. She swore she could feel him purr as he traced his tongue across her shoulder, following the tattoo down her chest and to her breast.

Her breath caught as Graham lifted his head to study her in the light.

"Exquisite...precious...rare," he repeated, no trace of teasing in his eyes. "All others pale beside you," he finished, cupping her cheek in his hand. "Not to mention you could kick their asses with one hand tied behind your back." Jiliana kneed him in the stomach. He smiled at her through gritted teeth. "And my ass. Remind me never to get on your bad side...not that you have a bad side." He gave her an exaggerated wink. "So, what should I teach you...hmmmmm?"

He palmed one of her breasts and the nipple tightened into a hard and sensitive peak. "I know," he added, bending his head to lick her neck once more. She trembled when his mouth moved ever closer to the knot of skin he now rolled between his fingers. She wiggled, hoping to ease the need that speared sharp between her legs, only to cry out in a greater want when Graham sucked her breast into his mouth.

The sensation was unlike anything she had felt before. His tongue swirled around her nipple, teasing...tasting. Jiliana's hunger grew desperate as he suckled her, his teeth nipping on the swollen tip as he moved his hand to pinch her other breast.

"Graham!" She mouthed his name in near desperation, biting her lip to keep from screaming so the entire camp would hear. She bit harder when he slid his hand from her breast down her stomach to grasp one thigh and pull her legs apart.

When the scent of her arousal drifted around them, Graham groaned and ground his hips against her leg. "Do you taste as exotic as you smell?" he whispered against her skin, his fingers parting the folds of her sex. "Will you let me taste you, Jili? Tongue that perfect flesh of yours until you beg me to never stop?" To her utter disbelief, he pulled away and looked her square in the eyes, waiting for her answer.

His sudden bursts of gentleness always caught her off guard. Brash, a braggart, with far more flippancy than was good for any man—Graham also possessed a deeply moving honor that turned up more often in his life than he would ever admit.

His brows drew together as she hesitated, his eyes turning a darker hue as the question hung unanswered between them. "Jiliana?" he asked once more, searching her face for any sign that she had heard.

"I trust you," she said, touching the back of her hand to his cheek. "You have never failed me before."

His smile could have stopped the wind. "And I never will...you know that, right?"

He kissed her then, that joyous smile never wavering until desire drowned out any other thought. She relaxed into his arms as his mouth trailed across her skin, slow and sensuous as if now he had all the time in the world. Jiliana shuddered when his lips tugged once more at her nipple. She whimpered when he took it deeper into his mouth, sucking at the knotted tip. She cried his name when his teeth closed around the bud of flesh, building in pressure until she felt a rising sting of pain.

To her surprise, the ache was welcome, adding a depth to her pleasure that had not been there before. In response, she pulled his head closer, hoping he would take the hint and bite a little harder. When he did, she shuddered, feeling the burn echoed in the ache between her legs.

"So you like that do you?" When he drew his mouth away, Jiliana moaned, turning until he could give her other breast the same wicked treatment, first sucking her nipple into his mouth before clamping his teeth around the swollen flesh.

If her need had been great before, it was nothing compared to the desperation that seized her now. The thought of him tonguing her there, deep between her legs where the want waited raw and savage, sent her further into the realm of dark arousal.

"Please." She didn't know what she was begging him to do other than save her from the growing sensations that threatened to pull her under.

To her consternation, he moved his lips to her ear instead, as if he was deliberately refusing to do what he'd promised. She would give him no quarter, Jiliana decided, her need making her surly and tense. Wedging her foot between his legs, she stroked him with her toes, keeping the pressure as light as his. But Graham was more the master at this game. He ground his cock hard against her foot, crying out once when she felt him jerk in a swift release.

"You don't know how I needed that," he told her, his voice rough and thick. "Now I can focus all my attention on you...at least for a while."

With that, he sat up and curled his hands around her knees, pulling her legs apart. Jiliana resisted, feeling too vulnerable...too exposed.

Graham ran one hand up the inside of her thigh and cupped it over her sex, the protective gesture both a comfort and temptation. "Let go." Although his words were soft, they were more command than request. The clear blue of his eyes calmed the clouded grey of hers as she allowed herself to relax and do as he'd demanded.

Slowly, she let her legs fall apart, gasping her need when he began to move his hand across her mound, slipping his fingers between the folds of flesh to touch her more intimately.

When his lips brushed her stomach and moved lower, however, Jiliana felt her hesitation resurface. "Graham, are you sure you want to do this?"

"Absolutely," he replied, his breath hot on her skin. "I have thought of little else for days." As if to reassure her, his next kiss landed at the very top of her thigh, his tongue trailing hot and wet over her skin.

"Oh!"

His mouth inched ever closer, driving her hesitation into a desperate anticipation...especially when he spread her slit open and dipped one finger into her body. Jiliana jerked again, the movement drawing his finger in deeper, her gate of jewels releasing a flood of moisture that slicked between her thighs.

Graham rumbled his pleasure, his thumb rasping over her golden pearl, teasing her clit into a throbbing mass of sensitive flesh. He slipped his finger free and drove it high once more, forcing her to grab a handful of his hair as she braced herself against a new storm of emotion.

He looked up at her, his eyes flashing with a fever she'd never seen. "Listen, little one." She loved it when he called her that. It made her feel beautiful, feminine and delicate. "After I have licked you to the point where you can barely speak—" he ran his tongue across his teeth in dangerous delight "—I am going to stretch this snug cunt of yours until your jeweled gate swings open wide."

When he held up two fingers she trembled with a glorious dread, remembering the massive size of his cock. But already she ached to accept all he had to offer...whatever it took she would willingly give.

"Are we in agreement?" He arched one brow and she swore she had never seen such a glorious man.

She held her breath, unable to do more than nod as her heart doubled its frantic beat.

"Humph. Better find that tongue of yours, I plan on showing you a whole new use for it later."

If her throat had gone dry before, it was like a desert now. She couldn't force a sound through it—until Graham lowered his head and took her with his mouth. Jiliana shook so hard as his tongue found her clit, Graham had to put one hand on her stomach to hold her to the bed.

"Mmmmmm," he murmured, the vibration of his voice rippling over her golden pearl. His finger burrowed into her heat as his tongue lapped her long and slow, the combined movements causing Jiliana to find her voice at last.

"Ahhhhhh…unnnhhhhhh…" She chewed on her lip in an attempt to stifle her screams until Graham moved his hand from her stomach and slid his fingers into her mouth.

"Show me how you would taste me," he ordered before returning to his play between her legs. His tongue stabbed at her clit, short fast strokes to match the beat of his finger pumping in and out of her body, higher and deeper with each new thrust.

Jiliana spread her legs wider until she was completely open to his touch, exposed and aroused as she had never been before. And when he replaced his finger with his tongue, fluttering the thick muscle inside her gate of jewels, she felt the screams begin again.

In near desperation she did as he'd ordered, swirling her tongue around his finger before sucking it into her mouth. Was this what he wanted her to do? Taste his flesh as he was tasting hers? The thought of taking his cock into her mouth broke down the last of her resistance. She turned her cheek into his palm, smoothing her lips across the calloused skin. Her body made its own demands as Graham's tongue continued to work its magic. He rasped it hard against her clit, faster and faster as her pleasure grew. Her hips moved against his mouth as if he had already speared her with his scepter, his fingers spearing strong and steady into the heat and wet of her sex.

Her breath stopped and blew out in a sob as the wave of release began. Her body tightened in expectation—ready, soaring, almost at the brink...and then as he had promised, Graham added a second finger.

This new invasion caused her to writhe beneath him on the bed, stretched and aching and crying out for more. When he withdrew and tunneled into her once more, she could not keep from screaming his name, the frenzied sound echoing throughout the camp for anyone to hear. "Graham!"

In response he dug into her again, his tongue rasping her tender clit. She couldn't think, she couldn't breathe as he twisted his fingers inside her. Jiliana had lost complete control as her body arched in release, the blaze of bliss shooting from her core to singe every part of her with its passing. She thought she would gladly die in his arms as her pleasure took flight and sent her falling into the abyss.

Graham remained solid as a stone, his mouth and fingers rooted in place, unflinching in their mission despite the force with which she came. He grunted when her elbow hit his head, tonguing her roughly as she continued to shake. She moved his hand to her breast, crying out again when he pinched the pebbled nipple.

"More...please," she managed to beg, whimpering when he increased the pressure, the hurt only adding to her pleasure.

For long moments she lay suspended in time, melting in the fire, floating in the flames...wanting to say she would stay with him forever if he could keep her in this state of joy where her secrets could never be more than a shadow.

Did she love him? As the thought rose, she felt a piece of herself withdraw...go scurrying back into the void, leaving her less than she might have been. She let it go, not caring at its passing. She still had this moment...this experience to finish.

When she braved a look at him, his expression was as smug as she'd ever seen it, his eyes alight with a frenzied pride. "Now for lesson three."

Chapter Seven

The bed wasn't big enough for what Graham intended next. Lifting Jili as if she weighed no more than a child, he rolled easily to the floor, pulling her on top of him. Her scent lingered on his skin, rich and heady like fine mulled wine.

And her taste—her taste had been as exotic as he'd expected. Kissing her soundly, he let her taste mingle between them. She opened her mouth eagerly, inviting him to explore. His cock stood stiff and hard, ready for Jili to take in her mouth. Turnabout was fair play, and Graham had always prided himself on being a fair and honest man.

He didn't need to urge her to touch him...already she'd fisted him through his breeches. Damn things, he cursed, who thought they were necessary anyway? He fumbled at the lacings himself, ready to tear them apart in utter frustration—he'd need a clean pair anyway, he reasoned, having come in them already—when he heard her soft laughter.

"As your squire, it is my job to see you attired correctly. For every occasion," she added, slapping his hand aside and turning to the work herself. When she bent her head to study the knots, Graham felt his need rise to a more painful level.

When she finished and let his cock spill free, he gritted his teeth and tried to breathe. She wrapped her hands around his flesh and stroked him in a long smooth motion, nearly making him come on the spot. He would never survive it if she actually—Graham froze at the first tentative touch of her tongue. Every muscle in his body screamed at him to let go, spill his seed in a rush of heat and glory.

But he refused to come too soon....not this time. This time he intended to savor every single second. He needed a distraction, something to do while she took him in her mouth. Think of jousting, he admonished, as Jili circled her lips around him. He jerked at her touch, his hips bucking wildly. He pictured the long length of the wooden lance sailing toward its target...making contact, thrusting through the ring—

Damn, shite, hell. This was not working at all. She lapped her tongue over the sensitive tip, teasing him to a greater want. He buried his hands in her hair and pressed himself against her mouth. "More, Jili," he begged. "Take me deeper."

"Arghhhh." He screamed when she readily obeyed. The woman was proving to be an excellent student. Not that he'd ever doubted it for a single—"Ahhhhhh, hellllll," he bellowed as her slick wet lips surrounded him.

He was ready to come. More than ready. In mere seconds she had sucked him almost past the point of no return, and he battled bravely against the release.

More distraction. More—he caught a glimpse of her perfectly rounded ass out of the corner of his eye and settled on an amazing plan. Why hadn't he thought of it in the first place? He grabbed her hips in both his hands and hauled her over his chest, spreading her legs apart so she perfectly straddled his face.

She squealed, the vibration pulsing along his length, the ache in his cock the most blissful of pain. Before she could pull her mouth away, he placed one hand at the back of her neck and clamped the other around her bottom, pulling her cunt within reach of his tongue.

She squeaked again when he licked hard across her clit, his own moan of pleasure now tickling her sensitive flesh. She sucked harder, he licked deeper as they battled for who could hold out the longest.

But Graham was determined to win this war. Slicking one finger in the wet of her slit, he moved to trace the tiny ring of her ass. Teasing, waiting to see if she would accept him. He lapped her clit in short hard strokes, feeling her body quiver in anticipation as he wiggled his finger around her tight entrance. She hesitated, her mouth stilling around his flesh as he held his breath and pushed the finger in.

She bucked and jerked her head, her whimper ringing through the air. He felt the strong muscle clamp like a vise around his finger, sucking it even deeper inside. She cried out again, wiggling her hips as if uncertain about this new assault...but never once did she tell him to stop.

He slid his finger out and felt her relax, tensing around him when he tunneled into her again. He kept his tongue glued to her clit, working it hard as he fingered deep into her virgin ass. "Take me back into your mouth," he ordered, briefly pulling his mouth away, his other hand guiding her head back to his cock. She did as he directed, sucking him in with a single swallow. When he thrust into her ass again, she moaned around his flesh, the rumble enough to send him spiraling toward completion.

He was coming. Oh God was he coming! His balls tightened, ready to explode. His cock was in a state of hunger he'd never known before, he was licking the most delicious woman he'd ever tasted and his finger was—

SHITE. Graham lost complete control when Jili found the opening of his own ass and snugged her finger through. A man wasn't supposed to—

But it didn't matter one damn bit what a man was supposed to like. Her finger slipped into him in a single thrust, high and deep, the sensation sending him reeling in pleasure. He jerked as he came, calling out her name, the sound muffled by her body and his tongue on her flesh. She did not pull away as he flooded into her mouth, lost to the feel of her accepting him completely.

He was as elated as he had ever been when Jili's body began to shudder. Graham's cock continued to throb as he returned to the task at hand. While Jili's lips remained soothingly wrapped around him, he let his own tongue stroke her over and over, his finger pumping high into her ass. She trembled, shook and screamed her pleasure into his flesh.

And when it was over, she tucked her head against his thigh, her breath slowing as the world came into focus.

Later, he moved them back to the bed. He knew he needed sleep. But he refused to drift off and miss any of their time together. Instead, Graham stared at nothing, Jili held tight against him. To his stupefaction, he was totally content and satiated. He'd only come once...well twice if he counted that very first spurt when she'd rubbed him with her foot—which he didn't.

In times past it had taken several women to ease his needs. Some shadow of emptiness always seemed to haunt him. He thought of his father and the mother he had never known. Had his father loved her, found this simple peace in her arms? Had he ever loved Finella or Sam? He fingered a swath of Jili's hair, touching it to his lips. Had any other woman's hair felt so soft? Or lips tasted so sweet?

Bloody hell. If he kept this up, he'd be writing horridly stupid verse like some simpering poet dressed in lace, waving a posy beneath his nose. He might as well chop off his balls and feed them to the pigs for all the good they'd do him then.

He blamed Llewellyn, bastard number one. If he hadn't gone off and lost his mind—getting married...Dunmores didn't marry! And then Allard had shown the same vast stupidity when he'd taken Jo for a wife. Idiots, both of them.

Well, he would never fall to the same level of foppishness. He would remain a Dunmore true to the very end. Once this tournament was over, he'd go back to the life he'd enjoyed before...with as many women as it took to keep him sated, if Jili decided to leave his service.

His mood sank like a stone in water. Where would he ever find another to take her place...as his squire, he assured himself.

She sighed and trailed her hand down his stomach. His cock stiffened as he thought of pleasuring her again. The taste of her lingered in his mouth. Although he hadn't told her, it had been years since he'd buried his tongue into a woman's cunt...not relishing the thought of who had come before him.

He rolled her on her back and spread her legs again, her whimper of acceptance making him grit his teeth as his hunger grew. But this time he wanted more than her hands or mouth...he wanted—needed—to feel the hot walls of her cunt clench tight around him as she came.

Would she take him now? Dare he even ask?

She opened her eyes and met the need in his. She nodded, shifting her body so he could roll on top of her and settle between her legs. He kissed her, slowly, one hand delving between her thighs to swirl along the swelling nub of her clit. She gasped her pleasure, her hips arching against his hand, her legs parting even more as he flexed his hips and nudged the tip of his cock against the dewy opening of her slit. She stiffened as he pressed himself against her, the tight opening of her body trying to adjust to his mass.

"Easy, little one," he mouthed against her lips. "Relax...I promise you can take me." Almost. Almost. Bit by tiny bit he began to breach the fist of her sex as she gasped and shuddered beneath him.

She was ready to come. He could hear her breath grow sharp and shallow...feel the urgency of her hips against his. Now...she was ready, willing, crying out his name as she fell over the edge—

And then all hell broke loose.

ॐ

"Two days, Rose," Snapdragon complained, holding tight to the neck of the fat country rat she'd managed to charm into giving her a lift. "Two whole days!"

Pansy rode a mangy alley cat beside her, and Rose lay exhausted on an even scroungier-looking dog. All three animals were under a mind-control spell, so they plodded amiably along together, despite the fact they continued to eye each other in varying shades of alarm and suppressed aggression.

The three fairies had finally made it to the tournament. The swan they originally flew on decided to dump them in the middle of a forest just hours after giving them a ride. It had taken them all that night and half the next day to find other animal transportation.

Now, after several hours of using precious magic, the fairies were exhausted, the animals close to breaking the charm, and they couldn't find Graham's tent in the temporary village that had sprouted up around the tournament field.

"We're almost there," Rose answered as she always did, her eyes searching desperately for some sign that they were near.

It wasn't easy threading their way through the maze of tents and buildings, especially since the animals kept trying to shake free of the spell, and the humans they encountered insisted on chasing them away every chance they got.

Snapdragon and Pansy were ready to wring Rose's neck, and poor Rose was almost ready to let them. "Wait," she added, pointing to a tent several yards away. "Doesn't that look like the Dunmore crest hanging on that pole?"

"Where?" Pansy craned her neck to see, her vision blocked by the larger body of the dog ahead.

Snapdragon couldn't see one blasted thing from the back of the rat. She hadn't been able to see a thing all day, and had finally grown tired of being the last in line. She poked the rat with her wand, sending the animal speeding around the cat.

The cat hissed and arched its back, sending Pansy tumbling to the ground. As she hit dirt, her concentration failed, releasing the cat from the spell. Instantly it leapt at the rat, and Snapdragon wasn't fast enough to stop it. The rat—its survival instincts greater than the mind-charm—darted away, scurrying under the feet of the dog with Snapdragon holding on for dear life. The poor dog would have been fine if only the rat had run beneath it, but when the cat followed, reaching up to rake a claw across its belly, the dog retaliated by biting the cat's tail.

The animals broke free of control just as they reached Graham's tent. The rat scuttled beneath the flap of the door, took a quick look around for someplace to hide, and jumped beneath Graham's cot, Snapdragon holding on for dear life.

The cat hissed, pounced, and jumped on the bed, digging into Graham's ass for support as it peered over the edge to watch diligently for its prey.

Graham, having had his bare backside shredded beneath the cat's claws, let loose a roar that could have woken the dead and hurled himself on the floor, dragging his poor squire with him. Jiliana—to her credit—didn't utter a sound, but her fingers searched the floor around her feeling for anything she could use as a weapon.

The dog barked in chorus to Graham's curses, forcing its nose under the overturned bed to look for the cat who smacked it soundly for its trouble. Tail tucked between its legs, it bailed back out the door, Rose still clinging to its back.

Finally, Pansy poked her head into the chaos, her fingers wiggling in a frantic pattern. In seconds, the rat toppled over onto its back, its feet sticking straight up in the air. Deprived of her sport, the cat circled the edges of the tent, found a half-eaten piece of cheese on the floor and wolfed it down before slithering out after the dog.

"Pinch me, Jili," the fairies heard Graham mutter in desperation. "Wake me up so I know I haven't died and gone to a worse hell than even I deserve."

Snapdragon floated to land on his very-well muscled stomach, her gaze never leaving the sight of his great horn still poking up proudly. "Is this the thanks we get," she demanded, her eyes wide in admiration, "for coming to save your glorious ass?"

When Jiliana peeked around Graham's shoulder to stare at the fairy standing on his hip, he tried to turn her head away. "Don't look. If we keep our eyes closed real tight, they might go away and leave us in peace. If not...we are doomed." When Pansy joined Snapdragon, he thunked his head on the floor. "Better yet, just kill me and get it over with...please, I beg you."

He took her hands and wrapped them around his throat.

Rose drifted calmly into the tent to take her place with the others. All three stared at Graham's quickly shrinking cock with expressions as proud as any mother's.

"If you do not leave this instant," he stated slowly and clearly, "I cannot be held responsible for my actions." He wanted nothing better than to kill them all. He ground his teeth together so hard his jaw began to ache in concert with his cock as the tiny horrors clucked and tisked in complete disregard of his emotional state.

"Ungrateful ogre," muttered Pansy, her lips turning down. Graham knew that look...it did not bode well.

"Ogre is right." When Snapdragon snickered, her eyes still glued to his now flaccid manhood, Graham grabbed his breeches from the floor and tucked them against his groin. He was not going to be the object of their perverted fairy fantasies.

Jili continued to gape at the creatures, her eyes as round as pumpkins. "Are they real?"

"Of course we're real, dear, and we've already met. That first day at Finella and Samantha's house. We were sitting there at the table, although you had eyes for no one in the room but our little Graham. I am Rose." She smiled politely. "And these are Pansy and Snapdragon." She pointed to each in turn who bared their teeth in terrible parodies of smiles.

"Don't worry," Graham whispered in Jili's ear. "No one in the family has been seriously hurt by them...yet."

To his dismay, her face showed more curiosity than fear...just like his mothers'. This was not a good sign, he realized in growing alarm. For some reason he had yet to understand, women and fairies seemed to actually like each other. His horror intensified when Jili smiled in delight.

"They are called *kami* in the east, and honored most highly.

Not that I believed they were real. How lovely to meet you," she added, nodding her head to each of them in turn.

"Thank you." Snapdragon sniffed and hovered to land on Jili's shoulder. "We have been days on the road trying to get here to warn you—"

"With no food...unless you count those sour berries Rose picked and made us eat." Pansy fluttered to the bed and fell down as if she was dying from exhaustion.

Graham's disgust grew in direct proportion to Jili's fascination. "Don't let them fool you," he warned, "they're as hardy as the rats they rode in on."

"Only one rat," Rose huffed. "We also had a swan—"

"Nasty horrid birds," Snapdragon interrupted.

"—three squirrels—"

"Those animals are so nervous, I don't know how they survive," Pansy said, raising her head quite easily for one on the brink of certain demise.

"—the dog and the cat," Rose finished, frowning at the others. "It has been a difficult trip."

Jili peeked over Graham's shoulder to see her clothes still soaking in the bath. "Graham, if you would bring me my chest, I could get dressed and bring us all something for dinner."

"Don't bother." Graham stood and grabbed another pair of breeches from his trunk before jamming his shirt over his head. "I'll do it. I have to be at Bert's by sundown, anyway." He poked his head out and glared at the setting sun as if he could stop it in its track. Damnation! He couldn't believe he had to leave Jili tonight...or any other night, for that matter.

His sappy thoughts sullied his mood even more, and he stormed out of the tent without a backward glance. Maybe he was better off at Bert's. At least there he didn't have to worry about making a fool of himself over a woman.

Chapter Eight

After Graham left her alone with the fairies, Jiliana donned her spare set of clothing and ran a comb through her tangled and still wet hair. She smiled at the one called Snapdragon. "You said earlier you were coming to warn us? About what?"

The little woman frowned and pointed to the one dressed in pink...Rose, Jiliana remembered. "Ask her. She's been babbling about danger for days now." Snapdragon floated to sit by the blue-dressed one on Graham's bed. "We were perfectly contented to wait and come with the rest of the family...but she insisted."

Rose bobbed her head. "I have good instincts. And it is our job to keep you safe."

Pansy sat up and nodded. "Chapter one, section one, rule one of the Fairy Charter states... *The guardian fae's first and foremost responsibility is to insure the safety and happiness of their charges, in so much as those charges are in danger of bodily harm or injury arising from outside influences that could possibly interfere with the correct and proper life that they are intended to live...notwithstanding the usual trials of disease, old age, death or any other difficulty arising within the standard norm of human existence.*"

"You had to ask," Snapdragon grumbled.

Jiliana, however, was impressed, her own instincts having

been on the upswing for days. "Then I am sincerely glad you are here...no matter what Graham says," she added with a wink.

Later that night, however, alone and edgy, Jiliana couldn't sleep. She rolled restlessly in bed until her thoughts forced her to get up and go outside. The three fairies snored from their pillows on a chest, exhausted from their adventures of the past two days.

She was still astonished the creatures were real, and even more amazed by Graham's dislike of the trio. A chuckle trembled in her throat as she pictured him naked and aroused with the tiny women standing gawking on his hip.

Grabbing some grapes from their leftover meal, she ducked out of the tent. A beautiful summer night greeted her. Stars blinked down from above, the air was soft and made musical by the cricket's song, and a growing moon lent a shadowy magic to everything.

The setting was perfect for lovers and fools, she thought with a shake of her head, popping a grape into her mouth. And she fit the last category as if she'd been born to it.

A flush heated her cheeks when she remembered the afternoon. How could she have behaved so wantonly...and loved every sinful second of it? Graham, the bastard, made it all seem so right, as if she was made to writhe like a concubine in his arms while he schooled her in pillow play and other amorous delights.

And she was growing too worried for his safety in the tournament. Men could be maimed during their matches, or killed, and Graham's lack of sleep would most certainly take its toll. He still refused to quit...his pride unwilling to let him back down from the prince's challenge.

What would the masters say? Love was a dangerous distraction. It made warriors vulnerable when they had too much to lose.

She'd never had anything to lose before. Her life had been given in dedication to her craft—she knew as well as any soldier she was expected to offer it willingly. And she had, many times over. But to face the loss of Graham...this was a thing she'd not taken into account. And if there were children—

Children? She had completely lost her mind. She would not have a child. She couldn't afford the risk.

Which brought her to another dilemma. She had almost let Graham take her today, thrust his jade scepter through her gate of jewels as far as it would go...and she had been more than willing to let him.

She was falling too fast. She was losing her edge. What would happen if she lost control? How could she ever explain so he would understand? When the tournament was over, she'd have to make other plans before she fell so far under his spell she forgot who she was and why she couldn't love him.

A beggar leaned heavily on his crooked stick as she reached the main square of the temporary village. She nodded in greeting and tossed him the rest of the fruit. He caught it with an agility that surprised her, but if one had to live on the handouts of others, she reasoned, one would have to learn to snatch them as easily as they could.

He bowed as she passed, never meeting her gaze.

A muffled scream came from an alley to her right. Without hesitation, Jiliana ran towards the sound, hoping against hope another murder wasn't already taking place. Her *katana* was already drawn when she spotted the two figures in the shadows.

"Please, my lord," begged a too-young girl. "Yer hurting me."

"Shut up." The man bared his teeth, grabbing a hank of her hair to force her to her knees. His other hand tugged at the

111

lacings of his breeches. "If you're a good girl and suck me off fast, you'll be done before you know it." He pressed her face into his groin, obviously enjoying her struggles against him. "Fight me and I will take you in a less pleasant manner."

"And how would that be?" Jiliana smiled, making the expression as bleak as possible while admiring the wicked curve of her blade in the torchlight that filtered through the alley.

The man stiffened and turned, but did not release the girl. "None of your damned business." His eyes narrowed in speculation as they ran over her form. "Unless you are offering to take her place."

Jiliana's laugh was brittle as she pointed her *katana* at his crotch. "Let her go. Do you know what a eunuch is? In the east, they geld men like horses...chop off their sac so they can be trusted to guard the emperor's women. 'Tis a very old and honorable profession. Would you care to try it?" She took a step towards him. "Of course, I am not trained in the proper removal of testicles. But I would be most willing to attempt it."

The first trace of fear crossed his face when she took another step forward, her sword still at the ready. With a curse, the man threw the girl to the ground, his hand reaching to draw his own blade. As the girl scrambled off screaming, several people gathered to see what the commotion was all about.

They stayed to watch in nasty delight when they saw the two swords crossed and waiting.

The man gave her a look that would have sent a normal woman running. "Do you know who I am?" he demanded viciously.

Jiliana matched him glare for glare and let her voice grow louder. "Why don't you tell us all who you are...good sir...so everyone can know who tried to rape a child. Please—we are all very interested." Her lips turned down, however, when she recognized the emblem sewn onto the shoulder of his shirt. *The prince's man.*

For the briefest of an instant, she thought the knight might actually do what she'd demanded. His mouth opened and closed several times as his eyes darted to the crowd and then back to her. At last, raising his hands and giving a short bark of a laugh, he tucked his sword away.

"I will not forget this," he whispered for her ears alone before he turned and strode into the night.

Jiliana forced herself to relax. The last thing she needed was to have a public fight with a nobleman—who was in the prince's service. She was already suspected to have been involved in the two other murders...the last thing she needed was to add another to her list.

"Get on with you," she admonished the curious. "There is nothing more to see." She replaced her *katana* in its sheath and strode off in the opposite direction, wanting nothing more than to be safe in their tent with Graham's hands touching every part of her...except Graham was gone, already guarding the prince in disguise.

ॐ

He watched the altercation with interest, allowing himself the briefest of satisfactions as he melted into the shadows. To know the weakness of an enemy was a power unequalled. He would use it to his advantage.

After returning to his lodgings, he knelt in front of the altar, the sweet smoke of temple incense heavy in the air. He had already finished two of the five sacred tasks.

Pride swelled in his chest as he prepared for the next

offering, unwrapping the tools reverently before presenting them for the spirit's approval. Two long, delicate blades gleamed in the candle-light—perfectly sharpened and ready for their task.

He took a weapon in each of his hands, rocked back on his heels and stood in a single graceful movement, already spinning the swords in a deadly arc around his body. For long moments he continued the dance, merging his energy with that of the animal whose fighting spirit he sought to appease, every gesture and movement effortless and controlled.

There was beauty in everything, he realized as the truth of it surrounded him. Beauty in the stalk, beauty in the strike. Until at last the pristine beauty of death. Even the pain was a joy to be treasured.

He slid one blade across his chest and reveled in the pleasure as the metal bit his skin. The smell of his blood mingled with the incense. He was almost ready. It was nearly time.

℣

"Tell me about your squire." Bertram rolled the dice across the table.

Graham smiled when the numbers came up short. "Too bad, old man, better luck next time."

He studied the prince across the table, wondering what the man had in mind tonight. The harlots had been dismissed, and the beautiful Lila was tucked safely away. The two of them were alone. Graham leaned back in his chair and settled his broadsword across his lap. Lack of sleep was beginning to dull his wits and he was determined to resist any temptation the prince felt inclined to offer.

"What do you really know about her?"

Graham felt his hackles rise as the prince refused to leave the subject. "Her family worked for Ladies Samantha and Finella. They were all murdered when she was a girl...she herself barely survived the attack."

"Raped, no doubt."

Graham let the sentence hang between them.

"Go on," the prince ordered in a slurred and surly voice. Without his women to keep him amused, he had been drinking far more than he usually did.

Graham hoped the man would feel like shite in the morning. He grinned and re-filled Bert's cup. "She was determined to be able to defend herself after that, and when no man in Westmyre would consent to train her, my mothers sent word to a friend in Eastshyre. Jili crossed the Black-Toothed Mountains with a small escort when she was barely thirteen to see if the masters there would take her."

"Obviously they did." Bertram dangled a gold goblet negligently in his fingers. "Quite a brave and daunting task for a child. How long has she been home?" He pushed a tray of fruit in Graham's general direction.

"She showed up four weeks ago." He wiped an apple on his shirt and ate nearly half of it in a single bite.

"Just in time for the tournament. Don't you think that's rather serendipitous? A coincidence," he added when Graham frowned. "Are your wits slowing after all?"

"Not that I ever noticed."

"Humph. You can't hold out forever, Duncemore." Damn but he hated when Bert called him that. "Sooner or later exhaustion will get the better of you and you'll slip up. Wouldn't it be more prudent to just do what I ask? Go home. Leave me alone." When the prince frowned at his half-full drink, Graham eagerly topped it off. "Do you know anything at all about her...I

115

mean, other than she screams like a banshee when you prick her with your famous horn?"

While he knew he flushed, Graham remained silent on the matter.

"What will she do next?" the prince prodded again, picking absently at a bunch of grapes. "A woman with her skills is wasted here in Westmyre. I doubt anyone besides you would hire her. Is she looking to snag a husband?"

Graham snorted. "That's where you're wrong, Bert. For your information, Jili plans on being the first woman ever knighted. She is training as my squire for that very reason. I'm certain she can do it," he continued excitedly. "You should see her fight. She knows things that have even brought me down on occasion. I would put her up against any man you name, and bet my fortune she bested them easily."

"Are you proposing a challenge?" The prince's interest sparked immediately. "I can't think of a thing I'd enjoy more than seeing your warrioress in action. What would you be willing to wager?"

Graham leaned forward in eager anticipation. He had finally found a way out of his nightly imprisonment. "Back into my own bed," he answered, daring the prince to take back the offer.

But Bert smiled serenely and held out his hand. "Done," he said when Graham took it in his own.

"I cannot believe you agreed to this without asking me." Jiliana glared at Graham who was leaning calmly against the fence with his arms crossed over his chest.

"What?" He shrugged his massive shoulders. "Just kick his ass fast, and we can sleep together again tonight." A darkling glimmer twinkled at the back of his eyes.

She flushed, the thought pleasing her more than it should have. She had been unbearably lonely without him these past few nights, and, in truth, would have done just about anything to get him away from the prince's influence.

Already beyond tired, Graham still refused to pull out of the tournament. Every time she broached the subject he cut her off with a wave of his hand. She remembered what he had told her about his mother—and the two women who had raised him as their own—and knew how much he wanted to make them proud.

A lesser man would have buckled under the pressure. Sir Graham, however, was proving tougher than the prince had anticipated. That thought made Jiliana smile. Despite the fact he'd gotten no measurable sleep for three nights running, he'd beaten the prince at the joust for the last two days straight. In His Highness's attempts to beat down Graham, he had indulged overmuch himself. Yet both men were severely off their game. Not a good sign as far as she was concerned. Exhaustion made men careless. Carelessness led to injury and indiscretion.

She glanced up at Graham's smug expression, wondering what the two men spoke of during their long hours together and if the beautiful Lila came to keep them company in the night. Jiliana frowned as the thought took hold. Jealousy was a rogue emotion. It brought no peace, only bitterness and heartache.

Her thoughts were interrupted by Graham's rumbling laugh. "If that's the best he can do—"

She turned to see the prince and his men come striding across the field. Graham bowed, the briefest of gestures, and Sir Bertram's face grew stern. Graham's smile, on the other hand, couldn't have been any brighter.

"Good to see you, Bert," he called, standing to his full height and blocking out a good portion of sunlight. "Have you brought your champion?"

"Of course." The prince motioned a scrawny youth forward.

Jiliana's stomach fluttered in doubt. This couldn't be right. "The boy has not even sprouted a beard," she protested. "He will not challenge me at all."

"Are you backing out?" Bertram's voice was deceptively smooth. "I would be more than happy to have your master's company again tonight."

She felt Graham stiffen beside her and swallowed down her pride. For his sake, if nothing else, she would go through with this charade. "Very well." She unstrapped her *katana* and handed the blade to Graham, her lips twisting in mockery as the youth took off his shirt. "I will fight fully clothed, thank you very much."

"Damn right, she will," Graham bellowed behind her. "Go get him, woman, and be quick about it," he added out of the corner of his mouth. "I have plans aplenty for us later."

"Would you care to wager a second night?" the prince calmly asked. "Unless you don't have as much faith in your squire as you have led me to believe."

Jiliana shook her head as Graham opened his mouth in glee. "Graham don't."

But he was already shouting out his answer. "Make it three, and you've got yourself a deal!"

"So be it." The prince's face betrayed nothing as he accepted Graham's enthusiastic offer. But she saw his deception, even if Graham didn't, and knew that whoever won the fight, the outcome of the day would not be to Graham's satisfaction.

The boy faced her, his fists lifted in the traditional boxing pose. His first punch was so slow, she could have run around him twice before it ever landed. Nevertheless, she waited until the very last moment to slip out of the way, blocking the blow with one hand, her other hand landing solidly against his ribs.

He fell to the ground, gasping for breath, his face turning a dull shade of red.

Jiliana knelt and placed her hand on his chest. "Breathe in and out slowly. Good," she added when his breathing steadied. She stood and helped him to his feet. "Next time, punch from your center. Pivot at the waist and aim behind me. Makes for a stronger hit with better follow through, hmmm?"

The boy nodded, bouncing on his feet like an idiot. Jiliana fought down a grin as she assumed her own fighting stance, knees bent, her hands held relaxed and open-palmed in front of her chest. "Again."

The boy, despite his silly bobbing, had listened well. This time his punch came twice as fast, straight towards her as she stepped into the strike, grabbed his arm and held it, while her other hand caught him beneath the chin, knocking him to the ground once more.

Although the prince looked more than ready to call the match, the boy was beginning to enjoy her teaching.

"Can I try it one more time?" he begged, jumping to his feet and raising his fists to the ready. "I would love to learn that last move," he said, his head bobbing up and down like a bird's. "What should I do this time?"

"This time you should stay down," came Graham's amused reply, "so my squire can finish her work."

"Yes, sirs," said the boy when the prince nodded in agreement.

Jiliana anticipated the next strike. She stepped forward before he'd barely moved, knocked his arm aside and spun behind him, both hands curling over his shoulders as she pulled him off balance and let him land on his ass with a thump.

"Enough!" The prince's voice broke into the silence. "So, Duncemore, your champion has won the day. You get to spend the next three nights in your own tent. Send the lovely woman to take your place," he added in an undertone.

Graham's expression froze as the other man's words sank in. He grabbed the prince by the throat, as if he would haul the man off his feet. Only Jiliana's timely intervention kept the scene from escalating into true violence.

"Remember who he is," she hissed in Graham's ear. "It is not worth your life."

She turned to the prince and studied him as a master would study a wayward student. "A wise leader would have been happy to find a truly loyal servant. By deceiving him, you have quite possibly lost the faith of the one man in the kingdom who would have given it without question."

Not a single emotion touched the prince's face. "I expect you in my tent before nightfall," he ordered, spinning on his heel and striding calmly away.

Chapter Nine

"I won't let you do this." Graham paced the tent, his hands curled into fists. "No matter what that ass says, I'll guard him again tonight."

Jiliana finished polishing her *katana* and slid it calmly back into its sheath. "The matter is already settled. You should have thought harder before you made that idiotic bet."

He glared at her from his towering height, his lips turning down in a perfect frown. "I know, damn it. Next time I won't trust the sneaky bastard."

Just as she had feared, Graham's faith in the prince had been shaken. She reached out to touch his arm. "Maybe it was his way of giving in without losing face. You get a good night's sleep, he gets to look like he's won big, and you can wipe the field with him tomorrow." She smiled in encouragement, but Graham was already shaking his head.

"I'm going with you."

"You most certainly are not." Jiliana wagged her finger beneath his nose. "If I can guard the imperial princesses of Eastshyre, I can guard a Westmyre prince."

"I'll bet the Eastshyre princesses didn't plan to talk you into sharing their beds." He kicked a gauntlet across the floor.

"So that's what this is all about?" Wishing she had the

strength to pick Graham up and toss him out on his sorry ass, Jiliana tried her best to keep her anger in check. "Your jealousy? Unbelievable...I should have known you'd come up with something like this. This whole fiasco was your doing, not mine, and now you'll just have to live with it."

"No I don't," he stubbornly insisted. "I am still the master here, and you will do exactly what I tell you to do....stay put!"

Deciding on another approach lest she do something stupid like knock his gorgeous head off, Jiliana said, "You haven't even had supper, and there is plenty of time until dark. Let me bring you something to eat." And a lot of ale to drink, she added to herself, hoping she could get him quickly drunk and nodding off to sleep. "I promise I'll come right back," she added when he opened his mouth to protest.

"I swear, Jili, if you do anything stupid, I'll—"

"You'll what?" She muttered something unfeminine. "I am neither your slave nor your property, and you cannot threaten to punish me like you would a child." She knew she had made a mistake when she saw his face light up. He grabbed her wrist and jerked her against his chest, capturing her other hand before she had enough sense to react.

"You might think you can take on any man," he said in a dangerous tone, "but I am not just any man." When she struggled he smiled, a satisfied twist to his lips. He had her held so tight against him she could not find room for a kick, and he was strong enough she could not wiggle her wrists free.

He pulled her with him as he stepped toward the bed, his eyes growing darker with each passing moment.

"What are you doing?" Jiliana was shocked to hear the thread of fear in her voice. He didn't know the beast he was unleashing. He couldn't know what she was capable of as Graham propped one foot on the bed and bent her over his knee.

When she belatedly realized his true intent, she flew into a rage the likes of which she had not felt in years. "I will kill you," she said in a voice that had made other men tremble, "after I feed you your balls one by one." But to her relief, the anger was hot, alive, passionate and raw. Not like the deathly calm she knew so very well.

How long could she trust herself? How long before the cold took over, driving out the woman to replace her with the thing she had never managed to control? Trying to swallow her anger, trying to keep her breathing steady, she clamped her mouth shut and glared at him through eyes as black as his bastard heart.

Graham had not so much as flinched at her threat, transferring her wrists to one hand. "You can stop this right now, little one. All you have to do is obey your master."

In defiance, she shook her head, desperately searching for a way to escape. The first smack took her by surprise, the palm of his hand landing hard against her bottom. She bit her lip to keep from crying out as his hand came down again.

To her absolute horror, a dark need began to burn between her legs. How could she be aroused by this humiliating treatment? Graham had broken his word, and while not forcing her into his bed, he was certainly forcing her to accept this brutal control.

And her treacherous body was throbbing in a growing want. She pictured herself submitting to his will, groveling at his feet like some simpering slave, swallowing her pride as she swallowed his—

Graham's hand came down again, and she fought against her rising hunger. What would it be like to have him take her this way—bleak and powerful as he forced her to her pleasure?

Her nipples tightened where they rubbed against his thigh, the sensation only adding to her desire and confusion.

She squeezed her eyes shut, her memories beating to be freed. Is this what had happened before? Had she wanted those men to take her? Had she somehow lured them on? Not fought back enough? Did she give in too willingly?

The first tendril of ice rippled along her veins. The beast uncoiled, cold and calm. Her thoughts froze into crystalline clarity, her body moving with a mind of its own. When he raised his hand to strike again, she arched her back and rose, the base of her skull landing solidly against his nose.

Graham swore in words she'd never actually heard, but loosened his grip enough to let her make her escape. His nose was bleeding, she noticed with a faint satisfaction, turning away so he would not see the blank expression on her face as she began to gather her belongings.

"Jili, wait." When she heard him take a step toward her, she whirled, her *katana* held steady in her hand.

"You will never touch me again." If she hated the bitter tone of her voice, she hated the sound of his even more. Pity mixed with shame. It was just as well, she needed the knowledge to give her the strength to leave.

"Jili, please."

She raised her blade to his throat when he took another step. Whatever apology he thought to offer was too damned little, too damned late. She blinked back her regret, refusing to let him see the pain as her emotions returned to close off her throat.

"I can explain." His words were soft as he reached out to turn her blade aside, but with an easy movement, she sliced across his palm, deep enough to break the skin. For the first time she saw him hesitate, his face a mask to mirror hers.

124

"Explain it to someone who has to listen, Sir Graham." She continued to keep her sword held high as she grabbed the handle of her trunk and backed toward the door. "As of this moment, I am no longer in your employ."

"Now you've done it." Graham forced himself to remain in control as Pansy, the blue-dressed monster, flew down to hover before his face. "I mean, we've seen you do some pretty dumb things...but this was stupid, even for you."

He picked up his helmet and hurled it at her, snorting his displeasure when she ducked easily out of the way.

"Don't you think you should go after her, dear?" Rose fluttered nervously above his shoulder.

"No, damn it, I am not going after her. Don't you dare say a word," he added when he saw Snapdragon's mouth open. "You heard her...she quit. She is no longer my responsibility."

"Only because you were dumb enough to spank her." Snapdragon smiled as she got her opinion in. "I'm surprised she didn't chop your hand off."

Graham glared at the cut. She had exhibited amazing control, he realized in bleak appreciation of her skill. Had she been any less a master, he could have been facing another round of stitches...or worse.

Not that he didn't deserve it, not after the way he'd treated her.

"What were you thinking?" Pansy demanded, landing on the bed beside him. "The prince is not an ugly man...not by any means, and you have practically thrown her into his arms." The admiration in her voice when she mentioned the bastard prince was enough to send Graham over the edge. He swatted at her with the back of his hand, realizing his mistake when he hit a solid wall of magic. He cursed splendidly as he felt the crunch of bone.

"Oh my." Rose raised her wand and the pain subsided, along with the mark across his palm. And while Graham might have wanted to thank her for her trouble, his aching pride kept his tongue silent.

Snapdragon's eyes gleamed with brutal pleasure. "She's going to be alone with Bert all night tonight. I'll bet he doesn't treat her like a child. I'll bet he treats her like a woman...a beautiful, desirable, pleasing wom—"

Graham didn't stay to hear the rest. Storming out of his tent, he went to find the prince. He would make the man see reason, even if he'd failed with Jili. A man understands these things, he reasoned with himself, and Bert was a man—even if he was a complete and total ass. Once he had Bert on his side, he would find a way to make Jili forgive him. He was Graham Dunmore, after all. No woman had ever been able to resist his charms for long.

But by the time he reached the prince's tent, Jili was already at her post and the man refused to see him. Grinding his teeth in frustration, Graham planted himself by the tent-flap, daring anyone to make him move. He heard the prince laugh and tell the guards to let him stay, his embarrassment nearly making him choke.

But he would not leave her alone with the man, no matter how it galled his pride. If she needed him, he would be there. Even if he had to give the princeling his wish and drop out of the tournament to do it.

Jiliana stood hesitantly in the prince's tent, taking in her surroundings. Where Graham had told of silks and pillows draped lavishly about, now there was only a simple table with two chairs in the center of the chamber. The rest of the tent was draped off with a curtain, and the prince sat facing her across the table.

"Your Highness." She bowed.

He frowned. "So the bastard told you who I am. How many others has he blabbered this information to?"

"No one, to my knowledge. Was he sworn to secrecy?"

"He may very well be."

"Then to his credit, he did not tell the entire camp. Few men would face you in the lists if they knew your true identity."

The prince snorted. "Call me Sir Bertram wherever we are. Less chance of you making a mistake that way. Sit down."

She straightened and did as he commanded, folding her hands on her lap and waiting motionlessly for whatever he had planned. It had taken all her effort to get the fight with Graham pushed to a back corner of her mind, and the prince's casual mention of his name brought all her pain and betrayal to the fore. Why had he acted like such a barbarian? As her anger rose, so did the void. She took several breaths, calming herself as best she could.

The prince smiled and leaned back in his chair, giving her a view of his thickly muscled chest as his shirt parted and fell down his shoulders. He was a handsome man, she acknowledged, with dark curly hair and piercing eyes to match. Those eyes studied her with a feral intensity, as if they could read her every tormented thought.

A lesser soul would have faltered beneath that heavy gaze, but Jiliana was made of sterner stuff. She looked back at him with a practiced detachment, knowing that to all outward appearances she seemed unfazed by his ruthless study and in complete control of the situation.

He was the one who finally broke the silence.

"Unbelievable...a woman who can actually hold her tongue. Wherever did Duncemore find you, and how can I possibly lure you away?" He leaned forward with his elbows on the table, his fingers steepled beneath his chin. "Are you oath-bound to him?"

"No."

"Prescripted for any particular length of time?"

"No."

"Then you are free to leave his service whenever you choose?" His smile grew friendly.

Jiliana refused to be drawn in by the comfortable expression. "I have already left his service." She regretted it the moment the words left her mouth.

"So you have seen reason at last?" Bertram chuckled. "My dear girl, no-one in your position would have willingly stayed with a half-trained knight who has wasted most of his life either drinking or whoring. What did he do, hmmmm? From what I— and everyone else in the camp could hear—the two of you had more than the average working relationship."

Although she felt the heat that rose to her cheeks, Jiliana kept her silence. Despite the fact she wanted to strangle Graham with a passion only matched by how much she wanted to be back in his arms, she would not give Bertram that bit of information.

She had already seen how the man had manipulated Graham before, and would give him no fuel to add to his fire. If anyone was going to send Dunmore to his maker, it was damn well going to be her.

"Not that I care who you fuck," the prince continued in a calculating tone, "or who you don't...although I could pay you better."

She smiled at this, honestly amused by his offer. Had he

known anything about her, he would have known she could never be bought with a few gold coins. Graham knew that, her treacherous heart stated calmly. Graham knew that and so much more.

And he betrayed that trust. Her rational mind came to the rescue, its cynicism a welcome defense against her heart's rebellious yearnings.

Bertram's eyes narrowed. "Do you find that funny? I assure you I am in earnest. What would you charge for a night in my bed?" Her continued refusal to answer seemed to irritate the prince for the very first time. "Wine," he ordered, his mouth thinning.

Instantly a very beautiful girl appeared from the back chamber, carrying a tray of wine and fruit. He sent her away with a flick of his fingers. Spoiled, Jiliana realized. As were all men of his station. However he tried to hide it, he was a man who had never heard the word no.

He took a swallow of the wine, his brows drawing together in annoyance before he masked the expression and smiled once more. He waved his hand at the second glass. "Drink."

She did not move a muscle. "Is that a command?"

"If you wish it to be." He had obviously changed tactics. Now a thread of seduction laced his words, kicking Jiliana into full guard again as she reached to do his bidding, sipping at the wine. "Perhaps I should be the one at your every whim and fancy. How would you command me, Jiliana? What would you have me do to win my lady's favor?"

"I am not a lady," she answered with a wry twist of her mouth, catching the telling gesture too late to keep him from seeing it.

His next words nearly caused her to choke as she took another drink of wine. "I could give you a title and lands of your own. Something very few women ever get a chance at. I have rewarded many men the same for their loyal service. Say the word and 'tis done."

"Why?" Jiliana frowned at him in true puzzlement. "Surely you have sycophants aplenty groveling for your favor. You have no need of me."

He stood and moved around to her chair, sitting on the table beside her, leaning close to whisper in her ear, his breath hot against her skin. "You are different. I have watched you training on the field. You fight better than most of the poor sods here—not that they have the intelligence to see it—and you are truly one of the most beautiful women I have ever met." He smoothed a hand down her hair, the gesture both tender and possessive. "Most men are fickle, their loyalties swaying with every turn of fortune...but once a woman has pledged herself, body and soul—" he tucked his hand beneath her chin and tilted her face to his "—there are few things in all the world that can make her change her mind."

Jiliana's heart was racing despite her best efforts to control it. He was offering her power beyond what she'd ever imagined. A knighthood, wealth, complete control over her life. Everything she'd ever wanted...and all she had to give up was everything she already had. No longer had, she amended, the magnitude of her loss sinking in for the very first time. She had lost her only friend. How could anything else compare to that?

As if on cue, a huge commotion began outside. Jiliana heard Graham's voice rise in pitch as he argued with the prince's men. Then a guard begged Bertram's pardon and asked for an audience.

The prince grinned and told the man to enter, watching every emotion that played across her face. "This should prove most entertaining."

The guard cleared his throat and tried not to stare. "Sir Graham has asked to speak with you." Jiliana noted the man's omission of any title or salute. Were these palace guards? If so, then any number of people could know the prince was here.

Bertram raised a royal brow in her direction. "Should we let the great oaf in?"

She gritted her teeth with the effort it took not to tell both men to sod off.

"Dunmore swears he will stay until the woman is allowed to leave," the guard added.

The prince's bark of laughter was overly loud. "Then by all means, tell him he may wait outside as long as he feels like it. But the woman stays with me."

Again, without a formal salutation, the guard bowed and withdrew. Seconds later, Graham's roar nearly shook the tent. Bertram's elation grew in direct proportion, and Jiliana was reminded of the novice students who made fools of themselves while trying to prove their worth to the masters. It was never a pretty sight. She took another sip of her drink, admiring the delicate flavor.

"Do you like it?" the prince asked as she put the goblet down. "'Tis a favorite of Emperor Shiruto. Made from the sweetest cherries in the land."

"The emperor is known for his excellent taste."

"And so am I." He finished his glass and poured another, leaning against the table with his groin thrust forward.

Jiliana felt her discomfort rise. If he tried to force her—she could be killed for lifting a hand against the royal heir. Perhaps she should have done as Graham had demanded...trusted his instinct instead of letting her pride rule. She and he were two of a kind, she realized, both too obstinate for either of their good.

Looking the prince straight in the eye, she let him see the distaste she felt. "I will serve you as any obedient subject of the realm...no more and no less. But I cannot and will not sell my loyalty. How could you trust I would not betray you to anyone who offers more?"

For a moment, his face took on an ugly expression, and she thought she had gone too far. Then it cleared and he looked at her with none of the seduction he had shown before. "Your Duncemore showed the same stubbornness. I am almost impressed...almost." He slammed his glass on the table and stood. "Every man—and woman—has their price, Jiliana. I simply haven't found either of yours yet."

She raised her chin and gazed at him squarely. "Loyalty can never be bought. You of all men should know that. Goodnight, Your Highness," she added when he strode into the back chamber without another word.

Moving to take her place by the door, Jiliana noticed he left the curtain open. A snap of his fingers and two beautiful women floated to his side, slipping the robe from his shoulders as they readied him for bed. Although she tried her best to keep her gaze averted, if she ignored them completely, she wouldn't be doing her job. The prince's safety was her number one concern.

She knew he studied her through half-closed eyes as the two women stroked and sucked him to full arousal. What was he thinking? What emotion lurked in that bold black stare?

Although the flush of embarrassment rode high on her cheeks, she refused to look away, some unspoken challenge daring her to watch him. Was this how Graham felt when the prince tempted him with the beautiful paid companions—this bleak need that settled like a weight upon her body? Every sound the prince made became Graham's voice whispering in her ear...every grunt of pleasure reminding her of the way she felt naked and trembling in his arms.

The bastard. How could he have betrayed her?

He did not force you, the voice of reason tried to answer. *Not in any way that you made him promise not to.*

So what? Her childish self butted in. He had used his strength and size against her.

And you liked it, added the woman struggling to emerge. *You have finally found a man who can best you on occasion, and you cannot deny you wanted nothing more than to yield.*

Chikusho. Although the curse remained unspoken, it reverberated in her head. Truth was a thing she had never taken lightly. She had always known that truth of self was a decidedly double-edged blade. You could not pick and choose which truths you would acknowledge. It made you blind to your darkness and dimmed the essence of your light.

The prince was starting to come. He kept his gaze locked with hers as his hips jerked and he fisted the courtesan's hair, forcing himself deeper into her mouth. His growl of release filled the tent as his body shuddered with the rush of pleasure. After he was spent, he pushed the woman away, patting her head as if she were no more than an expensive pet.

When Jiliana's lips curled in derision the prince smiled, showing he had noticed the weakness.

"Good night, lady," he said, giving her a mocking bow before lying down to sleep, seeming as satisfied as a bull at stud.

At long last, Jiliana's hunger ebbed. She sat cross-legged on the floor, her *katana* unsheathed and cradled on her lap, calmly alert as the night wore on. The prince lay still, his women curled on the floor beside him, giggling like silly geese before finally falling silent.

It took her by surprise when she saw a girl steal quietly from behind the curtain to come and sit next to her by the door. She was beautiful...very beautiful, with a tumble of luxurious blonde hair that fell past her waist, sparkling blue eyes and perfectly white skin. This must be the famous Lila, Jiliana thought with a grimace, wondering what on earth the girl wanted with her.

Lila smiled softly in the dim candle-light. "May I join you?" When Jiliana nodded, Lila dropped gracefully to the floor, her eyes serious as they searched her face. "You are not like the others."

Jiliana let her own gaze study the girl's, fascinated by the shrewdness she saw in the deep blue depths. There was intelligence here...and a sincere desire for communication.

"No, I am not like the others."

Lila sighed and rested her head against Jiliana's shoulder, the casual gesture a surprise. "Tell me about your life. What's it like to be free to do as you choose?"

Jiliana frowned in sudden understanding. Despite the girl's amazing beauty and poise, she was trapped like a fly in honey— a slave to the whims of her master, despite the richness of her cage. "How old are you?" she asked, smoothing a swath of golden hair that had fallen across her arm. "Where do you come from?"

Lila twirled another lock of her hair around her finger. "I am not certain. I know that I am of royal blood...but they will not tell me my family's name or why I was given to the prince to serve."

"Does every woman here know who he is?"

"No. Only me. The others are from Earl Rulfert's estate." Lila snuggled closer. "Your master was the first man I have ever been offered to."

Jiliana's thoughts betrayed her and she stiffened, but managed to force her breath to remain steady. "He refused."

"Mmmm." Lila's voice grew soft. "Not that I would have minded, he is beautiful." She blinked at Jiliana through her lashes. "If the prince offered me to you I would be most willing to obey..."

Her voice trailed off into a silence Jiliana refused to break. What would she do with the girl? She'd never in her life had a woman friend. She'd been the only woman of her age training at the school. All the others were so much older they'd taken no interest in the shy and gangly girl from the west. And she had never pressed for their friendship. She'd been there to learn to fight, and feminine companionship hadn't been on her list of necessities.

But she guessed Lila couldn't be more than four or five years younger than she was, although the differences in their lives made the gap seem so much wider. And she knew the girl was offering her more than friendship. Had she taken Jiliana's refusal of the prince as a sign she preferred another woman's touch?

As she began to glean the truth, Jiliana raised her head, feeling the prince's eyes fastened upon them from behind the thin curtain where he watched from his bed. She forced herself to smile before turning her head to whisper in Lila's ear, hoping the gesture looked more intimate than it was. "Did he order you to come to me?"

The girl's eyes flashed in amusement. She nuzzled her cheek against Jiliana's before whispering back, "It upsets his highness greatly that both you and your master have proven immune to his bribes so far."

"What do you want?" Jiliana whispered back. "Are you content to remain here?"

"I am content to do my duty to my master...as you are content to do your duty to yours."

She opened her mouth to assure the girl that Graham was not her master, but snapped it shut as a glimmer of truth began to wiggle into her awareness. She'd had many masters...teachers she respected enough to give her life for. And she had begun to respect Graham enough to add him to the list.

But she'd never considered herself a slave. She'd always served of her own free choice. Was serving out of love less binding than serving out of need? Jiliana looked again at the prince as Lila laid her head back on her shoulder. He wasn't a cruel man—not that she could tell—but he was a dangerous one. He had power, he had riches, and he had a unique ability for discovering and exploiting a person's weakness. He would make a great king...but could he ever be trusted as a man?

She thought of Graham's guileless personality. Where he was as open as the sky, the prince was as hidden as a mountain cavern. Not that she had need to worry. Mountain could never shut in sky...nor could sky ever uproot mountain, such was the nature of the two. But was there room for anything more? On some level the men balanced each other completely...but would either of them be willing to admit to the other's strengths?

Lila slept comfortably cuddled against her, and Jiliana felt an odd contentment steal over her, a companionship with the golden-haired girl that settled peacefully in her stomach. She could hear Graham's deep voice outside the tent, talking to one or another of the prince's guards, his joviality causing the men to guffaw as he told them one tall tale after another. Oh, she was still beyond furious at his ridiculous antics, but it soothed her stinging pride to know he was attempting to atone for his behavior...or so she hoped.

Whatever the new day might have in store, this night, at least, gave her a measure of peace she hadn't known in many months.

Chapter Ten

When the prince released her in the morning, Jiliana practically ran from the tent, dodging through the early fog in the hopes she could keep Graham from following. She wasn't ready to forgive him yet.

But she hadn't taken into account the man's utter single-mindedness of purpose. He had started snoring just before dawn, and although she tried her best to sneak by him, he woke as soon as she passed, like some mangy hound doggedly following her scent.

"Jili, please, let me explain." He grabbed her by the elbow as he caught up, his eyes red from lack of sleep and his face as fallen as she'd ever seen it. Not that she would be swayed by his remorse. He should have thought of that before he'd spanked her. She choked down the memory as her body began to stir, and jerked her elbow from his fingers.

"Don't bother. I couldn't care less." She ducked between two tents set very close together, allowing herself a smile when she heard him curse as he tripped over one of the support posts. She made another swift turn to her left, this time underneath a rope with clothes hanging out to dry. The sound he made when he ran into the line was music to her ears.

After making another quick turn, she looked behind her, smirking when she didn't see him anywhere. "Nice try,

Duncemore," she muttered under her breath, the words ending in a silent shriek when he appeared in the fog before her, materializing like some great ghost in her path.

"Stop right now and listen to what I have to say." He planted himself in the middle of her way, legs splayed wide and arms crossed over his chest. Like he thought that was going to stop her.

She spun to the left as if to move past him, and as he shifted his weight to intercept her, she whirled back to the right, barely squeaking around his leg. One hand shot out to catch her wrist, but this time Jiliana anticipated the tactic. Placing her other hand over his, she ducked under both their arms, the speed of her move throwing Graham so completely off balance she tossed him head over heels to land sputtering on the ground.

"Damn," he gasped in admiration, blinking up at her through his fabulous lashes. "You have got to teach me that sometime."

Without bothering to reply, she stormed off in a completely different direction, picking up her pace to a run when she heard him pounding behind her.

Anger turned to elation as the chase became a game of wills. Hunter and hunted, they fled through the dewy morning, past peddlers selling barley cakes and sausages...past the smith's forges, the leather-workers and the tailors, until they reached the edge of the fields where the horses were being fed and groomed.

Graham was fast, but Jiliana was faster. She pressed her advantage in the open field, slipping around the stable and behind a stack of hay, the dense fog aiding in her disappearance. There, she thought smugly, that should teach him a thing or two. Two steps took her through the back door of the stable, and she crouched in the shadows, listening for any sign that Graham had managed to follow.

No heavy footsteps approached, and she had just begun to catch her breath when a slip of movement caught the corner of her eye...a furtive flicker that touched off alarm bells in her mind.

It was followed by a muffled cry—an ominous strangled sound.

Jiliana drew her *katana* and made her way deeper into the stable, her own steps as stealthy as her prey's. Her feet made no sound in the straw. Toe to heel she moved as she had been taught, remembering her master's admonition as he spread the whisper thin rice paper across the floor. *"One must learn to walk in silence. When you make no mark upon the paper, you will have mastered the way of the tiger."* She took a breath and held it, letting her mind calm before she blew it out, breathing deep again as she let Tiger take over.

Her hearing sharpened.

Her sight sharpened.

Her smell sharpened.

Straw and horse mingled heavy in the air, along with sweat and leather. But underneath, faint and fleeting, was a scent that had no place among the animals and men of the west. Incense from the temples. Used by eastern warriors for centuries, its spicy odor cleansed the mind and calmed the spirit in preparation for battle.

Several squires tussled as they went about their appointed tasks, blind to the danger that stalked them. One boy lobbed an apple and hit another upside the head. The second retaliated with a ladle of water, drenching a third who stumbled into their path.

Good, Jiliana praised them silently. Stay together. There is safety in numbers. A summons from outside had the boys running to obey, leaving her alone again, searching urgently for a sign of the other intruder.

A flash of metal glinted from a dark corner, followed by another muffled scream.

She ran toward the sound, only to freeze as she stared at the man, bound and gagged, jerking in his death throws as his blood spilled out and pooled around him. His eyes had been cut out and placed in a bowl beside him, along with two other gory objects of a similar size and shape. The thick red stain between his legs hinted at their origin.

This had most certainly been done by the hand of man. With a growing dread, Jiliana recognized the victim. The prince's guard she had caught forcing himself on the young girl—the one she had threatened to castrate before an eager crowd of watchers.

If she had been suspected of foul play before, she would be certainly be charged with murder now.

Hearing the faint rustle of material behind her, she whirled, dropping to the ground as the *katana* sliced through the air above her head. She rolled to her feet, blocking the second strike just before it connected with her throat. Her opponent turned in the opposite direction, this time aiming for Jiliana's thigh.

She sidestepped, ramming her elbow hard into the assassin's kidney, following through with a *katana* strike to the upper arm. He blocked it, the grate of metal on metal making her teeth hurt. The sound of a second blade slicing through the air caused Jiliana to pivot just in time to dodge the deadly blow. Two swords against her one. The odds were not in her favor.

A trickle of serenity rippled through her—icy-calm and uncontrollable. The world slowed to a crawl. Her body relaxed as her inner savage took over. She could not stop it no matter how she tried. Her humanity receded as the killer in her emerged.

The stable door opened and a slice of sunlight illuminated the bloody scene. The assassin broke his concentration for the briefest of seconds, but for Jiliana, it was long enough. Swinging up with all her skill, her *katana* slipped unerringly through his defenses, biting into his shoulder until she felt her sword meet bone. Blood spurted from the wound, covering her with a thick hot spray. She shuddered with the force of her elation...her victory...her triumph.

Now. He was wounded, vulnerable, an easy target. She shivered with the rush of excitement as she drew back to strike once more. But not to kill...not yet. That would be too fast...too easy. Make him pay for his crimes as she had made all the others pay. Only through their fear and terror could the wounded beast in her find peace. She sliced low to his leg, cutting through skin, no more. She heard the subtle grunt of pain and smiled. He whirled out of reach as she aimed for his stomach, unable to connect.

He was better than she'd given him credit for, maintaining his discipline despite his injuries. Good. She liked it when they fought her, gave her a decent challenge. That made it all the sweeter when she finally took them down.

Voices called out in alarm as others raced to the scene. She didn't have time to play. He had to be finished before she could turn her attention to the others. *"Hai!"* The cry gave her strength and a rush of speed as she lunged, intending to slice his head from his body.

But her opponent was well-practiced in his art. She missed again as he rolled away, melting unseen into the shadows, to leave her standing over the corpse of the knight, her clothes and *katana* smeared with blood, battle-lust still singing in her veins.

"What trouble have you managed to get us into now?" she heard Graham demand, his tone heavy with resignation as men surrounded them in a menacing circle. "Do not say one word," he added, pulling her to his side, "until we are before Bertram."

Jiliana's rational mind tried not to resist his arms around her, but the darker part of her had yet to realize the danger was past. Her inner beast held more control than her mind, and although she warred against the movement, she turned on him, her *katana* raising to his throat, trembling in her grip as she struggled to pull herself from the abyss.

Graham's face took on a puzzled look. "Jili, for heaven's sake, give me that blasted sword. Do you hear me?" A darker expression settled over his features as his gaze bored into hers. Very slowly, he took a step towards her and guided her arm to her side. "Jili, damn it, stand down!"

At last his voice broke through the chaos that raged within her, bringing her back from the edge. She nodded, unable to form the words that would reassure him. His assessed her, cold and harsh—one warrior taking the measure of another. How much did he see, she wondered? Did he know how close she had come to destroying them both?

She did not resist when he led her through the crowd, the look on his face causing the throng to part like water before him. Yet despite the darkening outlook of her situation, Jiliana felt some small measure of relief. She knew who the enemy was, and she knew how to mount the counterattack. When the assassin was found and finally brought to justice, she would be able to prove her innocence.

And then she would leave before she could hurt anyone else.

ॐ

He stared at the blood soaked bandage wrapped around his arm. It angered him more than he cared to admit that the woman had nearly bested him. He would never have thought she was so highly trained.

In fascination, he bared his wound to the light. The skin and muscle were sliced cleanly through, with a precision even he could barely match. It would have been a pleasure to subdue her, he thought in unaccustomed regret, have her submit to his every demand.

But she was tainted. Stained beyond redemption. Once you left the way...there was no turning back.

Not even a grimace marred his calm expression as he picked up the needle and began to stitch the wound.

ॐ

"I did not do this." Jiliana was on her knees before the prince, her earlier confidence slipping as she saw the anger etched upon his face.

He held her *katana* in his hands, the blood dried and caked upon the blade. He was visibly shaken. "That man was captain of the royal guards. He has served my family faithfully for over twenty years."

"I am sorry." She could think of nothing else to say. Where she had seen a hunter of children, Bertram saw only a loyal employee. She doubted he cared what the man did on his own time. More the pity.

"You publicly threatened to castrate him, if I was informed correctly. Do you deny it?"

"No."

"And now he is murdered by that very same manner." He crouched and tucked a finger beneath her chin, studying her face from all angles. "Tell me, what would you think if you were in my position?"

"I would think," Graham butted in, stepping close to her side, "that things are not always what they seem."

A cloud lodged in the prince's eyes, a dangerous shadow that settled in hard as he stood and glared at Graham. "This from the man whose brother was recently involved in the disappearance of Duke Benedict Caryns and the murder of High Judge Tibult—all the while spouting some incoherent nonsense about black magic and shadow-monsters. You do see my skepticism."

Although Graham's face reddened, he refused to back down. "Both your parents and the church absolved him of any crime."

"Of course they did." The contempt in his voice was obvious. "Your mothers have always been too much of an influence. To hear my parents talk, we should all be one big happy family. Can you imagine? The Duncemore bastards in line for the throne."

Graham's gaze sharpened. "I assure you, Your Highness, that neither I, nor my brothers, have that ambition."

So, she thought. This explained a great deal of the animosity the prince felt for Graham. No man likes to hear others praised before him. Especially not one who would one day rule them all.

"But none of that has any bearing on Jili." There was a subtle warning to Graham's tone, as if he was making certain she wouldn't be used as a scapegoat. "At least hear her out...you owe her that much."

"I don't owe either of you a damned thing," the prince rejoined. "And, quite frankly, I am reaching the end of my patience. But I don't care to be accused of sending an innocent woman to the block."

The idea made Jiliana shudder. She was in danger here...if not for her life, then most certainly for her freedom. Even if she escaped back to Eastshyre, she would have to live in exile. She had already burned too many bridges there.

"You claim someone else attacked you. That you injured him. Yet not one of the several men who were there saw any sign of another person, although they locked the place down and searched it from top to bottom." The prince laid her *katana* on the floor and rubbed his hands across his face. "No one saw him but you."

"I did."

Jiliana and Bertram's heads jerked in unison at Graham's unexpected words.

The prince was the first to recover. "You saw him." Doubt laced his voice. "What did he look like?" His eyes marked Graham's every expression.

"A shadow."

"That just vanished into thin air?"

"You have no idea what a ninja is capable of, Your Highness," Jiliana inserted, not daring to meet Graham's gaze.

Bertram made an unpleasant sound. "I have heard the stories...that they can walk through walls and fly through the air. Bullshit, the lot of it."

"They make you believe they can," she asserted with a certainty born of experience, "which is just as useful a tool.

Your very unwillingness to acknowledge their existence proves they are masters at deception. They feed on fear and superstition and use them to their best advantage."

"Bloody hell." Bertram paced the tent, a wild animal ready to escape. "Do you see, Duncemore, what I have to deal with every day of my life? I cannot so much as leave the palace without becoming embroiled in deadly schemes and power struggles."

"You are the future king," Graham stated. "A man cannot change his birth."

For long moments the prince stared at them both. When he ducked out the door, he motioned them to follow.

"Sir Graham has vouched for his lady's honor," the prince stated to the gathered crowd. "Does anyone dare to challenge him?" Although there were mutters and whispers of discontent, not a single man stepped forward. "So be it. She is found innocent of all charges. Go away...have lunch, the games will continue this afternoon as scheduled."

"We should let Earl Rulfert make the decision," one man called from the back. "'E holds the highest rank."

"I will inform the earl of everything," Bertram assured, his authoritative manner calming the crowd. "I have sent word to him already. Is there anything else?"

Slowly, people walked away, glancing back at Jiliana as if she'd just grown horns and a tail. When most had retreated well out of earshot, Sir Bertram turned to Graham. "I hold you personally responsible for any and all of her actions. And do not think I will spare the noose if either of you are guilty of anything—no matter what our combined mothers have to say on the matter."

"Thank you, Your Highness." Graham was as serious as she had ever seen him. "Do we have permission to search for the murderer?"

"If you insist." The prince's lips twisted mockingly. "But how do you plan to catch a shadow?"

"He makes a good point," Jiliana said after the prince had retired to his tent. "A trained ninja will be nearly impossible to find."

"Not if you injured him as seriously as you think." Graham scanned the area in all directions. "If you cut through tendon, that arm will be noticeably damaged."

She snorted. "What do you plan on doing? Clapping every man on the shoulder to see which one cries out?"

"If I have to." He chewed his lip thoughtfully. "You know the ways of his people. If you were that injured, where would you go to hide?"

"In the place you would least expect to find me." She sighed and raised her eyes to his. "You didn't see him, did you? You lied to the prince."

Graham lifted one massive shoulder. "Only if you lied to me."

"I didn't."

"I know."

"Thank you." She glanced at him in true and utter frustration. In less than a day, he had pissed her off worse than anyone had ever done, yet stood ready to defend her with his life against the accusations of his peers. But she knew he would protect her and that made her even more afraid. He couldn't have a clue what he was getting himself involved with.

He ran a finger down her cheek. "About last night...I am sorry, Jili. I acted like an ass, and if you give me time I'm guaranteed to do it again. 'Tis a particular Dunmore specialty."

"I hated you for it."

"That you did." A half-smile tilted up one corner of his lips. "Did I mention how gorgeous you are when you're mad? I'll probably have to piss you off quite often, just to be able to gape at your beauty."

She tried her best not to return his smile. "You are an ass." But she couldn't deny that she was pleased by his flattery...which was exactly what he wanted, she admitted ruefully. Once a rogue, always a rogue.

"Then let me be your ass...I swear to always live up to the title." He reached out and tentatively tugged a lock of her hair. "What do you say? Come back. After this damned tournament is over, we can do whatever you want...wherever you want...whenever you want." One blue eye closed in an exaggerated wink.

Jiliana sighed. The man was a study in irritation. He was also strong, handsome, and made her feel things she'd never felt before. When she wasn't trying to kill him, she thought, they got along nicely. Already her body was begging for his touch—treacherous beast that it was. How would she manage to walk away?

She blinked against the sunlight. It held no easy answer. But the day was already well at hand, and they had yet to do their morning meditation. "Time for the *kata*." It would do no good to discuss the incident. It would not change what was to come. They walked to the field and assumed the first stance, flowing in unison from tiger to snake to crane to le—

"Why crane?" Graham frowned, gazing at his hands. "I mean, I understand the others, but how could some silly bird possibly fight off a tiger?"

Before Graham had a chance to react, Jiliana attacked, her finger-strike stopping just as she touched his eye. "Crane defends by pecking out Tiger's eyes. Tiger blinded cannot—" Her body froze as her mind raced over the possibility. Tiger to snake to crane...the bodies...tiger to snake to crane to leo—

How could she not have seen it sooner? How could she not have known?

"Graham, we have to go back and talk to the prince. He is in danger. Someone has hired an assassin."

She grabbed his arm and pulled him behind her. "The first body...mauled...killed by tiger. The second man...poisoned...killed by snake, and the third man...his eyes cut out...killed by crane. There are only two animals left—leopard and dragon."

"Whoa, woman." Graham rooted his feet to the earth, nearly knocking Jiliana off her feet as he hauled her back against him. "Slow down and explain this to me before we have to face old Bert again."

"The *kata*. We do it every day. It is made up of the five great animal fighting styles. Tiger, snake, crane, leopard, and dragon. But to the darker of the masters, those who practice *ninjutsu*—the assassin's art, they are the five animal forms of death." Energy charged through her like a lightning strike as she pieced the puzzle together at last. "I have heard rumors of a ritual performed by assassins who adhere to the strictest of traditions. One kill to appease each of the animal spirits, ending in the death of the actual target. Think, can't you see the pattern? All of the men were in the prince's employ. Each death seeming non-related to the outsider, but each murder performed in perfect sequence and precision by the attacker."

She knew the instant he grasped the truth. His eyes blazed in terrible understanding. "So he has to kill one more person before he can attack the prince? This might buy us a bit of time."

"Only because he is injured." Jiliana shuddered. "Leopard

eviscerates. It will be an ugly death...and someone much closer to His Highness."

Graham's face paled. "So if the dragon fighting style is a combination of all the others, then the prince's murder—" He swallowed. "I think we'd better pay Bert another visit, and hope this time he'll be happier to see us. But what about the last man's balls being chopped off? That doesn't fit the pattern."

"It does if you are looking to throw off the scent. He must have seen me challenge the guard. He knows who I am...even if I don't know a single thing about him." And that made her an easy mark. She would have to be more than cautious if she was to find him before he recovered enough to finish his job and let her take the blame—or worse.

Chapter Eleven

Snapdragon, Pansy and Rose fluttered nervously as Jili and Graham ran to find the prince.

"You heard her," Rose said, unable to keep the I-told-you-so out of her voice. "An assassin on the loose."

Pansy's expression was grim. "What can we possibly do? He's human. Without our scrying bowl or any magic to track, we are as useless as wings on a pig."

"I don't think so." Snapdragon wiggled her fingers and closed her hand around a long iron rod that materialized from the air. "You heard them. He's injured. Three fairies can poke a whole lot of shoulders," she said with a grin. "Big, muscled, knightly shoulders."

As if the fates were entirely lined up against Jiliana and Graham, the prince vehemently refused to grant them an audience. "Having tea with Earl Rulfert," they were informed by a rough-faced guardsman.

"Tea?" Graham hollered loud enough for the whole camp to hear. "Only women and buggerers have tea together. Which is it, Bert? Are you a woman or a—"

The tent-flap was pushed aside and the prince walked out, his face devoid of any emotion. "How nice, Duncemore. You have finally given me a reason to have your head chopped off. Say another word, and I'll have it done by an amateur...with a rusted blade." He smiled pleasantly.

"Please, Your Highness," Graham said, lowering his voice. "'Tis of the utmost importance. We have reason to believe your life is in danger...that you are the ultimate target of the assassin."

"More of your secret ninja warrior nonsense?" He glanced pointedly at Jiliana who'd had all of his sarcasm she could take today, prince or no prince.

"What will it take to convince you?" she bit back. "Who else needs to die for you to believe?"

Another man poked his head out of the tent. Earl Rulfert smiled. "The girl makes a good point, Your Highness." He said the title loud enough to make the prince flinch. "If your life is in jeopardy...mayhaps the girl could give us a demonstration. Show us how these ghostly killers are supposed to do their jobs."

Graham was already shaking his head. "She is not trained in...what did you call it, Jili?"

"*Ninjutsu.*" Her guilt rose up to choke her. She should have told him so many things. But if he didn't know the truth, he couldn't be hurt by it. He was innocent, that was all that mattered.

"*Ninjutsu.*" The word rolled easily from the earl's tongue. "Sounds very mysterious." He sidled close and patted her arm.

"And ridiculous." The prince shook his head. No one...and I mean no one...could get past my finest guards without them knowing."

"Are you willing to bet your life on that?" Despite her best effort, Jiliana's pride got the better of her. She had seen his finest guards...taking their duties all too lightly. If she'd wanted, she could have broken into his tent on numerous occasions. In fact, she'd contemplated it more than once to check that Graham was behaving like a gentleman while in the prince's service.

The briefest flicker of doubt entered the prince's eyes. "Show me," he said, not a trace of compassion on his face. "Tomorrow morning, when the sun is fully risen. And I don't want to see either of you until then."

As he turned in dismissal, Graham cleared his throat. The disbelief on the prince's face would have been comical if the circumstances were not so dismal.

"Yes?"

"Um...Your Highness...I would consider it an honor if... I mean I would be honored to..." Jiliana had never seen Graham have such trouble putting a sentence together. He swallowed several times, his face growing redder and redder. Even Bertram looked at him as if he were having some kind of fit.

"Bloody hell...would you allow me to quit the tourney and serve as your squire until the games are over?"

ᘒ

The earl burst in without bothering to knock. "You said you could handle it."

This interruption of his meditation caused him a momentary lack in discipline, anger flowing to the surface unchecked for several long moments. "I can and I will."

"Not that I can tell." The other man crossed and grabbed his shirt, tearing the delicate silk to bare the jagged wound beneath. "She is better than you, and you can't admit it."

He ground his jaw against another rush of rage, biting back the words of defense. They were a weakness he could not afford.

"Why is it taking so damned long, anyway?" Rulfert paced the chamber, sneezing when the smoke of the incense reached his bulbous nose. "And get rid of that god-awful stuff. I can't breathe in my very own castle." He opened the single window and gulped in air as loudly as he could. Not a pretty sight by any stretch of the imagination. "The prince knows."

He raised one finely plucked brow. "Indeed?"

"And he has agreed to let the girl prove to him that ninjas do exist." Rulfert gave him a contemptuous look. "You had your chance and failed. Now we do it my way. Tomorrow, when the demonstration starts, I want you to go to the prince's tent and kill two more of his guards. I will lead a group of men there and blame it on the girl. This time she won't have an alibi. With her out of the way, the prince will relax, thinking the danger is over. Do you think, with all your bumbling, you will be able to kill him then?"

"That is not in the ritual."

"I don't give a rat's ass about your ritual. I want the prince dead." The earl came close and nearly spat in his face. "You need to remember who is master here. If he doesn't die, you do."

As the other man stormed out of the room, he breathed deep, letting the spicy scent quiet his emotions once more. He would not kill—not outside of the ritual, but he could injure and he could maim. As for the final sacrifice before the actual assassination...he had already found the perfect target, and the fool would never see it coming.

౸

Ladies Finella, Samantha, and the rest of the Dunmore

clan arrived that afternoon. Jiliana greeted them warmly. The two women had looked out for her welfare very generously after her father's death, writing her letters during her long years away, keeping her caught up with their lives and the happenings of Westmyre.

Graham, however, shuffled his feet and stayed well back from the crowd of family that surrounded them. Lord Llewellyn, eldest Dunmore brother, stood with his wife, Lady Jessaline, holding their oldest child. Her belly was already rounded with their second.

Allard, second brother and now a judge on the King's Bench, stepped over to greet her and introduce his new wife, Jo. Graham had given Jiliana a brief history of Jo's background, and now that she met the woman, her respect grew by bounds. Sleek, toned, with a controlled manner to her words and expressions, Jiliana realized the other woman was as different from the norm as she was.

When Jo's mouth widened into a mischievous grin, her husband moved between them with a decided shake of his head. "I don't think so," he said, slipping a protective arm around his wife's tiny waist.

"You don't think so what?" she replied, wagging a finger beneath his nose. She winked at Jiliana before he began to pull her away. "I am certain the two of us will have many things to discuss. Can you really climb walls without a rope? That is a skill I would truly love to learn."

"I would be most honored to teach you." She couldn't suppress a smile when she saw Jo twist easily from her husband's grasp and pluck his purse from his belt before he had a chance to stop her. Their mingled laughter filled the air as he chased her through the crowd.

And lastly, Jiliana was introduced to Lord High Mason

Wynn Seville and his wife, Lady Jane. She remembered the *albhus* from her childhood—a strangely pale young man who was far too reticent even then. Through their letters, Finella and Samantha let Jiliana know he had matured into a man worthy of respect. She bowed her head before meeting his steely gaze with a calm one of her own, doing her best not to laugh when his beautiful wife insisted he put on a many-plumed hat to keep the sun out of his eyes.

To Jiliana's surprise, he acquiesced graciously, his mouth turning up in wry amusement as he doffed the horrendous head-dress.

Lady Jane was as warm as her husband was cold, the two of them forming the perfect balance of male and female principles...*yin* and *yang* as she had learned it in the east.

As they all moved to take their seats and watch the day's events, Jiliana gave Graham an exasperated glance. "Why didn't you tell them? Your decision was both honorable and selfless. They will be proud of the choice you made."

Graham frowned, looking everywhere but at her. "It stinks," he muttered, running his hand through his short-cropped hair. "This whole bloody damn tournament stinks. What will my brothers think when they see me squiring the prince?" He kicked the ground and spun toward the stables. "This has got to be the very worst day of my life."

Jiliana understood his frustration. She also understood that he was the only one in his family who would ever think less of him because of his choice. But she wouldn't even try to convince him of that. He would have to come to his own acceptance. Still, she felt his shame as if it were her own. She knew too much of pride. How it damaged. How it controlled.

Queen Amanda had arrived earlier that morning, and insisted the Dunmores sit with her to watch the day's events.

She smiled when Jiliana stepped into the booth and gave her a respectful bow.

Finella, however, frowned as Jiliana moved to stand behind her. "The fool didn't fire you, did he?"

"No, my lady. But I do need to tell you something. Graham has—"

The roar of the crowd drowned out her next words as Graham led the prince's horse out onto the field. Although his head was held high and his expression remained controlled, Jiliana knew how much it cost him.

Obviously his family did too.

"Oh, my." Samantha reached for Finella's hand. "I never thought when we asked Graham to watch out for the prince that Egbert would actually order him to become his man."

"Sir Bertram." Finella corrected. Her brow remained furrowed as she patted Samantha's hand reassuringly. "Tis what any man in his place would have to do, my dear. And our great big oaf has finally become a man."

Both women blinked hard, but only Samantha raised a finger to wipe a tear away. "I am prouder of him at this very moment than I have ever been."

Then they heard the first heckles from a row of young lords drinking the afternoon away.

"Oh, how the mighty has fallen. One knight squiring for another? 'Tis the saddest thing I've ever seen," called one. "What's the matter, Dumbmore? Chicken?"

Jiliana watched Graham's face turn a terrible shade of red. He kept his peace, however, saying nothing as he led the prince and his horse to present them to the lords and ladies in the booth.

"Hey, Great-ham...I need a slop boy," shouted another of

the youths.

"I could use an arse-wiper," mocked a third.

Graham's fist clenched reflexively and Jiliana willed him to remain calm. He did, standing with remarkable control as Sir Bertram smiled and bowed to all assembled.

"Does he keep your sword well-polished?" The first lordling stood to thrust his hips in Graham's direction. "Mine could use a spit-shine later."

As one, Llew, Allard and Wynn stood and lunged at the sullen youths. The men wore identical expressions that made even Jiliana shiver. She glanced at their mothers out of the corner of her eye to see both women's faces glowing with a joy they made no effort to hide.

"They are such wonderful boys," Finella gushed as Llew picked one man up from his seat and threw him over the railing.

"So well-bred," Samantha added as Allard cold-cocked a second, very likely breaking the young lord's nose.

"And Wynn has learned to be just as gracious." Finella's eyes flashed in anticipation as the last of the fools tried to run away from the white-skinned man. Wynn didn't have to say a single word to cause the youth to wet his breeches. After that, he tossed the lord onto the field with his two companions.

"Shall we challenge them to a duel?" Llew asked casually, slipping his sword free.

Allard shook his head. "Oh no, brother, I think it would be much better if the queen gave Graham permission to reclaim his honor. What say you, Your Royal Highness?" he called. "Shall Sir Graham be allowed to have recompense for his insults?"

By now the three idiot lords were looking for any possible

way to escape. One tried to make a run for it, but Wynn snatched him by the collar and lifted him easily from the ground. "And I am half the size of Sir Graham," he remarked in a very surprised tone as if the thought had just occurred to him.

The queen seemed to consider. "Sir Bertram, what say you? Should I allow your man the right to fight above his station?"

"That depends." He looked at Graham and then at the three youths. "He would have to take them all on at once...we couldn't have the tournament held up overlong." Then he sighed and shook his head. "We'd have to tie up one of his arms to make it an even battle." He frowned at Graham. "And blindfold him." Shrugging, he looked to Llew for support. "Would that be enough, or do you think we'd better cut off one leg, as well?"

By now the crowd was roaring in laughter as the other two lordlings loosed their bladders.

"If you want the boys to live," Llew replied, "we'd better take off both legs."

"And possibly both arms," Allard interjected. "Just to make it fair."

The prince gave an exasperated snort. "We really don't have time for this right now. But please give Sir Graham permission to exact any revenge he chooses when the tournament is over." He paused and moved his gaze slowly across the crowd. "From any man who dares to ridicule him," he added in a voice that rang with authority.

"So be it." The queen turned her eyes to Graham. "You are hereby, from this day forward, granted royal permission to defend your honor against any man who insults you...regardless of their station."

Absolute silence greeted this pronouncement. In a single

sentence, Graham had been given an unprecedented boon. Even Finella and Samantha exchanged startled looks.

But the prince seemed oddly pleased as he bowed to everyone from where he sat atop his horse. Jiliana's instincts sharpened wildly as she stared at Graham, who led the prince to his side of the yard. Lord Llewellyn, Allard and Wynn returned to their seats, whispering in delighted chagrin.

"Shite," Allard said, hitting his brother on the shoulder. "Better not piss him off now. He'll knock your head off, and I couldn't arrest him." His grin was honest. "Guess I'll have to suck up to him now instead of you."

Llewellyn roared with laughter, hugging his wife close. "Then we better be damned certain to put Wynn in the middle. He's the only one Graham is even remotely intimidated by."

Wynn's tone was wry as his lovely lady slammed his hat back on his head. "May I just say, for the record, that I can outrun you both."

Just then, Earl Rulfert came huffing into the booth. He bowed to the queen, pressing a quick kiss onto her hand. "Forgive me for being so late. I had another matter to attend to."

Jiliana watched him through lidded eyes, her ears alert to catch every word that was said.

"The match hasn't started yet," the queen answered pleasantly. "Sir Bertram is just about to whip Sir Herbert soundly." She glanced around in interest. "Where is Reginald? I would have thought he would be with you today."

The earl's mouth turned down. "My nephew has steadfastly refused to attend the games. He has assured me he has no time to watch men playing stupidly at war."

A breeze floated through the booth, bringing with it an all too familiar smell. Jiliana's head shot up as she tried to follow the scent, but it was gone before she had any chance to catch it. Nevertheless, she continued to scan the crowd as the prince and his opponent readied for the first pass.

A flicker of gold caught her eye, and Jiliana saw Lila, waving excitedly from her seat a few rows over. Jiliana waved back, the girl's obvious delight at seeing a familiar face mirrored in her own response.

It was getting harder and harder to contemplate a future alone. But she had no other choice. In disappointment, she turned away and concentrated all her attention back to Graham, the prince, and the danger at hand.

℘

By evening, Snapdragon, Pansy and Rose were frustrated, exhausted, and ready to blast something into smithereens. They had spent hours in the hot summer sun, poking every shoulder they could possibly find, and starting half a dozen fights...many of which had exploded into melee combat.

Tensions were high, tempers higher as they floated to land on a table in the square. A side of beef was roasting on an open pit, the smell of the meat making their stomachs growl. A minstrel plucked the strings of his lute before launching into a merry tune while the inevitable group of dancing girls fanned out among those come to watch.

"Well, that's it," Pansy said, smacking the dust from her gown. "Half the shoulders in the entire kingdom, and not one of them the one we were looking for."

Snapdragon glared at a group of half-soused knights. "Did we check them yet?"

"I don't remember," Rose mumbled, dropping her chin in her hands. "They've all started to look alike."

Snapdragon snorted. "And they stink." Her fascination with the burly men had long since faded. If she never saw another bulging muscle, it would be far too soon. Dragging her stick up one last time, she flew sluggishly toward the men, giving the first a nasty poke.

"Hey," he yelled, turning on the knight beside him. "Wot was that?"

"Wot was wot?"

"You hit me."

"Did not."

"Did to."

When Snapdragon poked the other man she was forced to duck the punch that landed on the first man's nose.

"Bastard," he bellowed, swinging back. But his buddy stumbled out of the way, and the punch split the third man's lip.

"Ass-wipe!" This knight attempted to draw his sword, but the weapon proved the smarter of the two, refusing to leave the protection of its sheath. In a growing rage its master unstrapped it from his belt, and beat the other man over the head.

Somehow, in the middle of all the chaos, Snapdragon managed to ram her rod into the last knight's shoulder. He jerked up his head so fast, he fell backwards into the roasting meat, screaming as he hit the hot coals. His friends pulled him out, laughing as they watched him run to a watering trough and sink his backside in.

The last of her strength fading, Snapdragon fluttered back to sit with her companions. "Done, and we didn't do one blasted thing." Her face fell like a half-baked cake.

Rose reached over and patted her arm, her own face not

nearly as disappointed. "Yes we did," she stated, looking to where the Dunmore family sat eating with Jiliana. Graham and the prince were no-where to be seen. "We know who the assassin isn't, and that will make our job so much easier.

"Now what?" Pansy wiggled her toes in her sweaty shoes. "I want my favorite slippers. I miss my room, our house, and the sound of bluc-bclls in the garden. Do you think we'll ever get to go home?"

Rose sighed, wondering the very same thing. "When we get finished here, we'll take a good long rest. If we don't use much more magic, we ought to be ready in a few months or so. In the meantime..." her eyes lit on a huge cherry tart, "...we'd better eat to keep up our strength."

℣

This is going be good, Graham thought, watching the prince smile in his direction. He had spent the entire evening checking over every inch of the man's armor and weaponry, looking for anything that might possibly have been sabotaged. He said nothing as Bert plucked a knife from his belt and tossed the blade from hand to hand.

"Graham Dunmore. I hardly know where to begin with you."

Graham stiffened, his teeth grinding together despite his best effort to stop the telling gesture.

"I have tried to bribe you," the prince continued, his smile broadening with every word, "wear you down, and have made no secret of my continued displeasure at your resistance."

Graham forced himself to put the prince's sword away, lest he do something stupid like drive it through the other man's heart. Bert laughed out loud as Graham slammed the blade into its sheath.

"I have insulted you publicly, and have practically accused you—and your lovely warrioress—of murder. Do you hate me yet?"

"Of a certainty, Your Highness." Graham bowed his head in respect.

By now Bert was laughing so hard he could barely draw breath. Graham smiled grimly and began to polish His Royal Ass's boots.

"And yet," the prince resumed, his expression turning somber as his gaze took on a biting intensity, "you passed every test I could come up with, and I find there is no man in the kingdom I would trust more with my life. Why is that, Duncemore?"

"My winning personality?" Graham finished the boot and sat it carefully on the floor before picking up the other.

"I am regretting this more by the minute." The prince shook his head in frustration and pointed to the ground at his feet. "Kneel."

Fighting back a slew of rude remarks, Graham did as Bert commanded. This had been his choice—to serve the prince, no matter what it cost him. He would see it through to the end, no matter how it galled his pride.

He frowned when the prince rolled up his sleeve and motioned him to do the same before he handed the blade to Graham. "Pledge your life to me. Not as a subject to his king," he added when Graham opened his mouth to say the words. "That oath is not worth the breath it takes to say it. Men change their allegiances as often as they change their whores, you know that as well as I do."

The truth settled like a weight between them.

Graham sliced the blade across his flesh. Blood welled up in a thick red line. "How, then, shall I give you my word?"

"As brother to brother." When Graham raised a brow, the prince nodded. "You Dunmores may be bastards...but never once have I known any of you to break your word." The prince dragged the knife across his own arm, making a cut nearly identical to Graham's and held out his arm.

Graham placed his against it and the pact was sealed. Blood to blood—a bond neither man could break.

In all his days, Graham had never heard of such a thing. Despite Bert's arrogant handling of the matter, the prince had pledged his life to Graham as surely as Graham had to him. There was no hierarchy in the blood-oath—it made both men equals within the sanctity of the bond.

As their gazes locked in a war they both expected, Graham was the one who surrendered first. "Well, well, brother," he said, his grin as twisted as he could make it, "you don't have a clue what you've gotten yourself into. I intend to make your life as miserable as I have made Llew and Allard's. And I promise I will enjoy every perfect second of it."

The prince frowned, his voice tightening to match Graham's. "Try it you pig-headed ass...I can't wait to see your head on my mantle."

"After I save your worthless life."

"Agreed." The prince's shoulders slumped in the only sign of vulnerability Graham had ever seen, and he wondered how it must have felt to be that alone, with no-one you could trust.

He fully understood how much faith the man had placed in him. It was an honor beyond anything Graham had ever aspired to. It was an honor he would defend until the very last breath he took.

"According to Jili, these ninjas command an exorbitant

price." Graham returned to polishing the prince's boots with a whole new sense of purpose. "Who could afford that here?"

"Only one man." Bert shook his head in genuine regret. "He was the one who suggested the tournament, and he was the one who offered to sponsor it, despite my parents' protests. He swore to defend me with his life if they allowed me to compete."

"The queen did not believe him."

"My mother has the instincts of a lion. I listen to her more than I ever admit."

Graham knew the feeling. He stood and strapped on his sword. "'Tis never easy to find you've been betrayed by one you once called friend."

"No." The prince's smile was nasty. "I have a cunning plan, Duncemore. One that will make your head spin with its ingenuity, and reel the fool in like a fish on a line."

Graham chuckled, liking this new situation better all the time. "I cannot wait to hear it, bro—"

Both men froze when the sound of feminine voices carried into the tent, their strident tones drowning out all rational thought.

"Bloody hell," Graham muttered, ducking his head like a boy.

"Our mothers are here. Put your sleeve back down," the prince added, rolling his eyes in dread. "I don't suppose you would kill me now and get it over with?"

Graham's smile wasn't pleasant. "Not a chance, brother. If I have to face them, you do too." The prince's smile was as forced as his as both men turned to the three women standing beaming in the doorway.

"Come in, ladies," Bert said, his tone as slick as polished marble. "Sir Graham and I were just saying how much we were looking forward to your visit."

Damn, Graham thought in true admiration. The man was good....very good.

Chapter Twelve

Jiliana tucked her hair beneath her shirt and pulled the black scarf over her face. She'd traded in her *hakama* for a pair of tight black breeches tucked into soft black leather slippers. The black shirt and scarf completed her attire.

"Where did you get those clothes?" Graham tried to stifle a yawn. Although he'd managed to get a few hours sleep yesterday, he had guarded the prince again last night. Given the suspicion surrounding her, she couldn't blame Bertram one bit.

"We were all given them at the school." She tied the leather straps of the *ashiko* over her boots. The spikes would allow her to climb without a rope, and could also be used to make her kicks more deadly in combat. "For night training." She should have told him from the beginning she knew more of the assassins' arts than she'd let on. It was too late now. Three men were dead, and Graham had already lied to the prince to protect her. Better he remain ignorant of her shady past.

Graham's brows drew together, but he didn't contradict her. How much did he suspect, she wondered, tucking a small knife into each boot and a few *shuriken*—metal throwing stars— into a hidden pocket of her shirt.

She still didn't know if she'd made the right decision in agreeing to the demonstration, acknowledging that her pride had played more than its fair share in the choice she'd made. Her masters would not have been pleased...not that they'd been pleased with any of her decisions in the end.

The student must learn that arrogance is the enemy...it clouds the mind and causes one to believe they are greater than any other. Pride slays many a foolish warrior.

Had she let her arrogance make up her mind? Wouldn't it have been best to concentrate her energies on finding the ninja, rather than proving to these men of the west that the assassins were made less of legend than of skill? She had no qualms about giving the ninja's secrets away. The more that was known about their dark and subversive ways the better they could be fought, so she'd agreed to Bertram and the earl's suggestion.

But all the while she knew that some part of her wanted to see Graham's face shine with pride when she showed them all she was telling the truth.

He glared at her now across the tent. "You don't have to prove anything to me...or that asshole Bert."

Jiliana crossed her arms over her chest. "I know this might not be the best way, but I have to convince them that ninjas are real and can be caught. If a *woman* can actually elude them, they might be willing to look for another suspect besides me."

"I can protect you." Graham's voice held such an air of conceit, she wanted to smack him.

"I don't need your damn protection. I don't need anyone's protection. Why in the hell do you think I've worked my butt off training these past few years? So that what happened to me before—"

She bit off the sentence and turned away, unwilling to let him see how her past still held such power over her emotions. Another conceit her masters found fault with. *The past should be let go like water flowing to the sea. Only in the release can one find true freedom.* She kept herself trapped in a prison of her own making.

When Graham pulled her close, she fought against the urge to let his strength become hers. For the briefest of an instant she allowed him to hold her, needing the physical contact. It was a comfort she'd rarely experienced and she'd grown to relish the feel of his arms around her. It would be a memory all too soon.

"I'm ready." After making certain she had everything she needed, Jiliana strode from the tent with Graham following close behind.

The sun blazed overhead, wheeling its way toward mid-sky. The stark daylight left little concealing shadow. Jiliana kept her eyes alert for any place that might offer cover, knowing that anyone who saw her would give away her presence. A line of thatched roofs marked the hastily erected buildings and stables, the only solid footing above, although some of the larger tents might be strong enough to hold her weight.

A sizable crowd had gathered near the jousting fields, and again the doubt nagged at her mind. This had become too public, too much like an exhibition. She was certain the assassin was watching from somewhere at the edges of the throng, much more aware of her actions than she could be of his.

And he'd never find a better time to strike. While the entire population was focused on her, he would have unfettered access to whomever he desired.

She had two tasks to accomplish. Find the ninja while keeping Bertram's men from finding her.

"Well, well, well." His Highness's amused voice broke into her musings. "I must say, Duncemore, she looks delicious dressed like a man. Is this how you take her, pretending she's some bare-faced youth?"

Jiliana watched Graham's face turn an interesting shade of purple. But to his credit, he held his temper somewhat in check.

"Ah, Bert," he mocked, slapping the prince hard on the shoulder. "At least I just pretend. My sword has always been kept in its proper scabbard...not thrust blindly into any sheath available."

Snickers floated from the crowd. Now it was the prince's turn to smile the barb aside. "Methinks her sheath would be an excellent place to have my sword's length polished."

"I think," Jiliana interrupted in a voice meant to freeze even the basest of replies, "that any honorable man would have the decency to spare the humble sheath the embarrassment of having to hear such remarks against her character."

Despite the shame she could not help but feel, Jiliana was proud her voice was stern and in command. Both men silenced although they continued to throw each other glances that were as deadly as any sword.

"Have you chosen your men?" She let her gaze roam the faces of the crowd. Anyone would think she was looking for the ones picked to track her, but she was searching for someone else entirely.

Bertram motioned four men forward. Jiliana turned her attention back to the task at hand.

"Earl Rulfert and Sir Herbert have volunteered for the demonstration, along with Lords Ferrall and Jarmen from Portlyn."

The four men gave her dutiful nods. Jiliana studied Sir Herbert, whose sullen face held a wealth of animosity. Obviously they both remembered their previous encounter. He seemed eager to name her the killer.

Graham grunted. "Got all your toadies lined up, did you?" He stopped in front of each man and glared down at them from his substantial height. Jiliana found her lips trying to smile when the two young lords actually backed a step or two away.

"They will do, Sir Graham." She gave him a confident smile when he turned around to face her. "Please, if you will give me a minute or two of silence, I will be ready." She heard the prince explaining to the onlookers exactly what was planned, from the length of time she had to evade capture, to the various tracking skills of the men he had picked. She let his voice fade as she willed herself to focus. Make no sound...leave no trace for them to follow. She would have no head start, no lead in her favor. As soon as she ran, the men would follow.

Smoke and fog. I am that which melds with the shadows, unseen and undetected.

Bertram motioned and the horn blew. Jiliana fled through the edges of the camp, the four men hot on her tail. She raced into the jumble of tents, weaving in and out of the men's sight, never getting too far ahead, never letting them come too close. Finally, she doubled back behind them, hoping to catch them off-guard and have a laugh at their expense.

She began to worry, however, when the men weren't where they should have been.

She'd left plenty of clues for them to follow. Her goal had been to keep them close enough to find her in an instant if she needed, but when she climbed to the uneven rooftops, she saw them rushing off in another direction entirely, led by the red-faced Rulfert.

Something was wrong. Jiliana followed, making no effort at all to hide as she jumped from roof to roof. It didn't take her long to see where they were headed—Bertram's tent.

And it took even less time for them to sound the alarm.

Jiliana watched in horrid fascination as the bodies were carried out and laid upon the ground. Two more of Bertram's men had been wounded...not killed, she realized in relief when one of them groaned and tried to stand.

Other men came running, voices shouted, and she heard her name called on more than one occasion. Graham and the prince squared off against each other, their expressions equally outraged and furious. A shove, a punch, and it took nearly a dozen men to pull the two apart.

As the scene continued to unfold before her, Jiliana remained frozen on the rooftop. She had played right into the enemy's hands. The only option she had now was to find some proof she wasn't the one they were after...even if she had to remain in hiding until she'd found it.

She thought of Graham's steadfast belief in her and cringed. He would bear the brunt of the prince's anger, his honor at stake, his life laid on the line. She had no other choice.

And if she failed...if she was truly unqualified for the task handed to her, she would return and trade her life for his. She understood the risk. She accepted the consequence.

Stubborn and prideful she might be, but Jiliana had learned her lessons well. If pride was her greatest sin, so be it. She would use that pride to fuel her determination. She would also use that pride to carry her through should the outcome prove not in her favor.

A single breath calmed her. A second cleared her mind and allowed her to view the scene again with a cool detachment. If she could control it—if she did not go too far over the line, she could become as dangerous as the one she tracked.

After all...it took one killer to think like another.

Sir Herbert's face was twisted in outrage as he drew his sword as if he would defend the entire camp. His expression reeked of sincerity and concern. He would likely run her through and ask questions later. But he was loyal to the prince and would make a formidable opponent.

Or sacrifice. The ritual was not yet complete. There was one death yet to come before the prince would be targeted.

Then why had these men been attacked? They had not been killed for a reason, she realized belatedly. They were not part of the assassin's plan. They were a distraction, meant to turn all suspicion on her. Someone had set this all up ahead of time.

She turned her attention to Earl Rulfert of the pleasant and amiable demeanor. He had enough money to buy himself the crown if the need should ever arise. Even now his expression hardly wavered. He stood, just to the side of Herbert, the same placid expression as before plastered upon his face. And as Jiliana watched, he took a tiny step back...and another...and another, until he had separated himself the slightest bit from the chaos around him.

What she saw next caused her heart to pound. Raising his hand as if to wipe the sweat from his brow, he made a gesture Jiliana had seen many times.

It would take someone familiar with the eastern art of war to pass on the secret language—and someone with those exact same skills to interpret it.

Jiliana let her gaze follow the path of Rulfert's hand. There! On a tent-top not far from where she perched crouched another motionless figure. He made a signal back and slid silently to the ground, running off in an angle that would take him clear of the gathered crowd and the clusters of people thronging to the scene.

Like a ghost, she followed him step for step, her own footprints fitting perfectly in his. To casual eyes it would appear as if only one person had traveled here. She fervently hoped that Rulfert would lead the chase for her in a completely different direction, believing only his man had escaped undetected this way.

When the man disappeared into a makeshift hovel at the very edges of the camp, she cursed as she saw the walking stick leaning against the side of the hovel. She had seen that beggar more than once, stumbling slowly down the streets as if he could barely move. Wasn't the best place to hide always in plain view?

If she hurried, she might catch him while he was changing. Despite the grace with which he moved, Jiliana had slashed his arm severely the last time they had met. Those trained in *ninjutsu* felt the same pain as any other, took the same amount of time to heal. She wouldn't be fooled by appearances again, not when she had been trained in the same techniques. Illusion was a powerful tool, but it didn't change the laws of the flesh.

Wishing futilely that she had her *katana*, or even her *ninja-to*, the much shorter sword made for concealment, she crouched next to the hut and took stock of what weaponry she did have. Four *shuriken*. She was quite skilled in throwing the deadly metal stars. Two small knives tucked into her boots. She pulled them out and stuck one in her mouth, holding the second knife in one hand, her *shuriken* ready in her other.

As she listened for any movement behind the thin wall, she tried to remember which arm she had injured before. His sword arm, she recalled...but something—she frowned as she struggled with the image—something had been unusual.

That was it! He swung his sword with his left hand. Many ninjas used this tactic to surprise their opponents, but his blows had flown too smoothly for that. Whoever the man was, he'd been born left-handed.

Before her mind had even registered the action, she hurled the *shuriken* at the left arm of the beggar who exited the hovel. But her aim had been too low. Instead of hitting his shoulder, it stuck deep into his forearm, spinning him around to face her.

A deathlike smile froze on his mouth as the two of them finally met eye to eye. Jiliana drew back in confusion and shock, her hand poised in mid-air unable to deliver the blow as he calmly pulled the *shuriken* from his arm, letting his blood spill freely to the ground.

She had met this man. Where? When?

As she hesitated, he threw something small and white at her face. *Metsubishi.* The egg-shell exploded when it hit, flinging sand, metal filings and pepper into her face. Her arm moved too late to protect her eyes, and she never saw the wooden cane that crashed into her skull. She went down on one knee, keeping her knives ready to strike. If she was lucky he wouldn't attack her with poison...if she was lucky.

But her earlier strike must have taken its toll. She smelled the sickly stench of blood and felt her shoes slip on the newly wet earth. Two bouts of blood loss in two days would weaken anyone.

With a muttered curse, he stumbled against the hovel, and she could hear him struggle to catch his breath. Jiliana still could not open her eyes to see what he would do, although she could feel him slowly move away. The smell of smoke teased her nose, and she realized he had set the hut on fire.

Chikuso! He was burning away all traces of his existence. There was no way she could search the burning hovel...no way she could prove another was even here. Except for the blood, although if they were to find her, they would quite likely assume the blood belonged to the two wounded guards.

Her head shot up as she heard the alarm go out.

Fire.

She could not escape. She fought back the rage that raised its waiting head. She could not let it overtake her now....she could not afford to lose control.

Graham was the first to reach her. "Damn it, Jili, are you all right?" He grabbed her by the arms and pulled her to her feet, running his hands over her body to see if she was injured.

"Not...mine," she managed to say. "The hut. Is it still standing? Can we get in?" Her hands were pressed tight against eyes that burned as if a thousand tiny daggers had been driven deep into them.

"No. 'Tis already gone. If anything was in there..." He let the sentence drop. "What happened?" He demanded in a rough voice.

"I found him, Graham. The assassin. He's been disguising himself as a beggar and working for Ru—"

"Shut up." He startled her into silence. "The prince and the others are coming. Whatever you do, do not mention anything you just told me. Do you understand? Swear to me, Jili, that no matter what, you will trust me and not say a single word. Now!" He ordered.

She didn't think she had ever heard him so deadly serious. Or so utterly frightened for her safety. Despite his harsh words, Jiliana heard the concern threaded just below the surface. Trust him. She had always trusted him, why on earth would she change that now?

"I swear," she whispered as the first wave of the crowd reached them

"'Tis her...she's the one," she heard Sir Herbert accuse. "Been missing since this whole thing started."

"We followed her footprints," Sir Rulfert added in a steady

voice. "Only one set. Look at her shoes, no-one else has even seen boots like those."

Jiliana knew he referred to her *tabi*, the split-toed footwear worn by ninja warriors. Her trick of following the assassin's footsteps had done nothing more than add to her apparent guilt.

"What say ye?" Sir Herbert demanded, sliding his sword-point beneath her chin to lift her face for them all to see.

Although Graham stiffened at her side, he made no move to stop the action.

"Not so impressive now, eh?" Bertram's voice dripped venom. "Good. Well done," he continued. "The girl is captured and will be locked up until she can be tried and hanged."

After blinking several more times, Jiliana managed to crack open her eyes and take stock of her situation. The crowd muttered its approval and her blood turned cold...especially when she heard Graham's heated reply.

"You bastard!" He lunged forward, swiping the sword from Herbert's hand as he faced off against the prince. "This is all a plan to get your filthy cock in her...just like you've wanted all along. That will never happen," he added, leveling the blade at the other man's chest. "Not as long as I draw breath."

The prince's face grew bleak. "Careful, Duncemore, that you can back up your stupid words."

"Oh, I can back them up, my friend. In fact, I'll bet my life on it. Shall we settle this on the field of honor?"

Jiliana struggled to keep her tongue. Despite the promise she had made to Graham, this was beyond all acceptability. She opened her mouth to protest, but clamped it shut again when she saw Graham's tightly closed expression.

"I accept," Bertram said. "We will meet tomorrow

afternoon."

"This cannot be allowed to happen." A regal voice came from the crowd. People parted as if by magic as a tall woman strode purposefully through the path that opened before her. "My son will not duel...not today, not ever."

"'Tis the queen," whispered Sir Herbert, dropping to one knee. "Your Royal Highness," he stated, bowing his head over her hand.

"Mother." The prince bowed in respect, but an even icier look took root in his eyes.

A thick silence settled on the crowd, the expression on each and every face the same. The prince! Sir Bertram was the prince! The secret was out at last.

The queen glared at both men. "Sir Graham has no authority to challenge you, Egbert."

The prince bared his teeth. "Of course he does, Your Majesty. You gave him that very right just yesterday."

Her head snapped back. "Then I rescind the pronouncement."

"You can't." It was as if the prince took a dark delight in her consternation. "The challenge was made first. With or without your approval, Sir Graham and I will fight." He bowed to his mother before bowing to Graham. "May the best man win," he calmly stated.

༚

Jiliana tossed on the simple cot, the chains around her ankles clinking as she moved. They had sent the prince's *chirurgeon* to wash out her eyes and tend to the scratches that covered her face. Her skin was now slathered with a green and foul-smelling paste, but that was the least of her worries.

Trust me, Graham had whispered once more when he handed her over to the royal guards. In the hours that had passed since then, she hadn't heard a word from him.

She had been fed—quite well, she acknowledged, looking at the fruit, cheese, and bread on a metal plate by the cot. Not that she'd managed to eat much. The events of the day had left her emotions adrift on a sea of confusion. How could she explain Graham's unfathomable behavior? Alone, arrested, in pain and in the dark, her thoughts began to turn in completely childish directions.

Was he drinking with the prince, taking his pleasure with any number of the beautiful courtesans available? No, couldn't be. She forced her mind to remain clear even as an exhausted sleep swept over her.

The duel. Graham and the prince had challenged each other, their rivalry spiraling out of control as tension and fear took over. Not even the queen had been able to stop it, she remembered, her heart hammering again in her chest. And she had been the cause.

But why should she wait like a lamb led to slaughter when she still had other options?

"Don't think you can keep me here for long," she promised both men as she fell into a dreamless sleep.

Chapter Thirteen

"Don't you dare do this!" Jiliana grabbed Graham's arm, refusing to let him strap on his sword belt. "This is barbaric, a ridiculous practice that should have gone out with the dark ages."

"'Tis the law." Graham jerked away, refusing to meet her eyes. The evasion made her hackles rise all the more.

"He is the prince, *baka,* you cannot possibly win this fight."

When he finally turned to face her, his eyes were a dark and anguished blue. "What would you have me do? Let them take you away? Hang you?" He shook his head and touched the scar along her jaw, the gesture so tender it almost proved her undoing. She swallowed, refusing to give in to her ever growing fear.

Jiliana hadn't been truly afraid in years, but now the emotion threatened to consume her. Her mouth felt like a desert and her heart beat so fast she could barely breathe. She couldn't think of a single word to say as Graham bent to brush his lips across her hair before striding from the tent to where certain failure waited—and death.

She knew with an overwhelming certainty that he planned to trade his life for hers. Just as certainly as she knew she would find a way to stop him.

Looking at the chains that bound her to the ground, she

saw the heavy metal spike embedded so far in the dirt she could not hope to pull it out. Not that she had any intention of wasting her time on the impossible. She concentrated her attention on the cuffs that encircled both her ankles and the surly faced guard that slouched in a chair, obviously put out that he would not be there to watch the show.

First things first. She sat with her back against the tent-post and forced her eyes shut, leaving them cracked the slightest bit so she could watch the man's every move. She let herself slowly slump as if sleeping, slowing her breath and forcing her body to relax.

And all the while she lulled him with her thoughts, letting images of peace and security drift through the air between them.

'Tis fine, she is sleeping. Exhausted from the strain. See, she is only a woman, weak like all the rest. You could step out for an instant. Tell the other you have to piss...be right back. No worries, she isn't going anywhere.

Over and over Jiliana threw him the thoughts, slow and patient as the masters had shown her. Over and over and over until she finally heard him stand and walk quietly to the door, shooting glances at her all the time as he convinced himself she was truly asleep.

When he slipped outside at last, she remained motionless for several long moments, her caution justified when another guard poked his head in to check that all was as it should be.

As soon as the tent flap fell into place once more, she untied the sash from her pants, slipped off her boots, and wrapped the material tight around one lower leg and foot—and even tighter still until she could feel the blood flow begin to cease. This served two purposes. The bindings would make her foot smaller and give a smoother surface to slide the metal against, as well dulling the pain as she worked her foot through the heavy metal cuff. It scraped her skin even beneath the roll of cloth, but she refused to get sidetracked by the pain. Luckily the bonds had been made for a man and even on their smallest setting were the briefest bit too big to hold her.

She got her first foot free and repeated the process, thanking any goddess who might be listening that the men of Westmyre were still so addle-headed they thought women incapable of either brains or brawn.

Even the prince for all the time he'd spent with her had continued to underestimate her skill...or had he?

Jiliana frowned at the disturbing thought. Too few men to watch her...shackles too large to hold her. Did he want her to escape? Give him a chance to kill her and be done with it, save the time and trouble of a public trial and hanging?

It didn't matter. Dead was dead, however it happened. She would make her last breaths count for something. She would make certain Graham was protected. She had made many mistakes in her life, most she regretted, some she did not...but to have Graham harmed because of her was not a guilt she would carry to her grave.

After walking a complete circle around the tent and listening carefully, Jiliana was certain only two guards remained, and they stood next to each other by the door of the tent. Shaking her head in disbelief, Jiliana slid beneath the heavy canvas of the back wall.

When she was free at last, she headed toward Bertram's tent.

Since the prince's own men had been sorely decimated, he had hired several of the knights at the tournament to stand guard in their stead. And this group was as lax as the other, thinking her captured and safely locked away. Instead of being alert and wary, they were placing bets on who would win the duel.

Stupid. Jiliana shook her head. If she had been in charge of training these men, they would be whipped for such frivolous behavior.

Nevertheless, it worked to her decided advantage now. Soft as a sigh, she moved to the back of the tent, dropped to the ground and crawled under the canvas.

The prince smiled at her when she stood and turned to face him. "Ah, Jiliana, what took you so long?"

Trying not to show her surprise, she gave him a small bow. "Sorry to disappoint you, Your Highness. Next time I will work faster." She spied her *katana* on the table and moved steadily toward it, returning his smile with a pleasant one of her own.

The prince, however, saw through the ploy and picked up the blade, balancing it on one palm. "A most magnificent weapon. Beautiful and deadly, just like the woman it was made for." He gave her a piercing look. "Have you come to slay me?" He laid the sword down and leaned back in his chair. "If so, then I have gravely misread your character."

She made no other effort to retrieve her weapon. "I have come to offer you my life in exchange for Sir Graham's."

"Of course you have," Bertram replied with a shake of his head. "Just as that oaf has offered his in place of yours. Damn stubborn, the both of you." He gave a humorless laugh. "But your loyalty is beyond contestation. And well deserved on both your parts. Come out, Duncemore, I know you cannot wait to say I told you so."

Graham practically leapt from the other chamber, an amazingly silly smile plastered across his face. "I told you so, Bert," he said, slapping the prince hard on the shoulder.

Jiliana frowned at them both. "This was all a test?"

185

"Uh, not all of it," Graham said. "Most people out there really do believe you're guilty. I just had to find a way to prove to my buddy here that you weren't."

"If I was guilty," she said, her gaze chastising the two men, "both of you would be dead by now. I had more than ample opportunity."

The prince arched one very regal brow. "You don't think I was ever stupid enough to believe Rulfert's ruse? But, in truth, he had to think I was. There was no other way to keep him feeling secure until I got the proof I needed to have him arrested."

Jiliana picked up her sword and slammed it into its sheath. "And now you have the proof?"

"No." Bert laughed. "I don't. Which is where you come in."

Graham moved to give her a quick hug. She shrugged off the touch, unwilling to forgive him so easily for allying with Sir Bertram against her. "What do you want me to do?" she asked the prince instead.

"While this huge fool and I are battling it out on the field...and my men keep your escape secret—" He smiled when he saw her look of surprise. "Yes, they were on to you the entire time, but ordered not to aid you in any way—you did have to prove you were an able ninja." He poured himself a glass of ale. "As I was saying, while Graham and I go toe to toe, you are to sneak into Rulfert's castle and find me something I can use to have the man arrested."

"There is still the matter of the assassin." Jiliana helped herself to a drink without asking the prince's permission. While he gave her a warning look, he refrained from any comment. Graham reached for a drink himself, grinning smugly the entire time. Again, the prince let the incident pass.

Graham was the only man in the entire kingdom, she

thought, who could afford to take such liberties with the future king of the realm. It made her heart swell with pride to know he had earned Bertram's respect at last.

Graham, however, didn't seem quite as amused as before. "You can't send her there on her own."

"Why not?" Jiliana and the prince spoke in unison. "I am the only one here who could possibly face Rulfert's assassin," she added, the shaken look on Graham's face tugging at her spirit. "I will be as swift and deadly as a tiger...I promise."

While his eyes remained clouded with worry, he finally nodded his acceptance.

"And we will be the ever-so-visible distraction." Bertram stood and smiled wickedly. "Squire, help me with my armor." He never took his gaze from Graham, and even Jiliana had to chuckle at his bemused expression.

"You don't really expect me to—"

"That is exactly what I expect, Duncemore, and don't you dare forget it. You came up with this scheme in the first place...you will make all the necessary concessions. 'Tis an order," the prince added gleefully, "if that makes it easier to swallow."

Graham's grin grew feral in return. "Just remember, we're supposed to make this look real...brother. And I can pack quite a wallop without damaging you in the least."

Bertram snorted. "I seriously doubt you'll manage to land a single blow. I have studied your technique, and can predict every move you make." He waved to a small chest Jiliana hadn't noticed before. "You should find everything you need in there, my dear...at least that's what this bastard claims. Did he manage to get it right?"

Her smile was as deadly serious as either of the men. "Perfectly," she answered, opening the lid. It was time to get to work.

&

"Can you see them?" Snapdragon stood on tip-toe and pushed Pansy out of the way.

Pansy dug her elbow into Snapdragon's side and made some progress in regaining her perch atop the roof of the royal booth where the queen, Finella, and Samantha had gathered to watch the scene play out.

The three noblewomen sat in rigid silence as they waited for their sons to meet on the field.

Rose shook her head and fluttered up to resume her place with the other two fairies. "We're going to have our hands full today. No matter what happens, we have to keep those two idiots from killing each other. Don't they know they're supposed to be friends?"

Snapdragon snorted. "I've been asking Pansy the same thing for years. She's never gotten the point, either."

"Right," Pansy retorted. "Like you are all fuzzy and warm inside."

Snapdragon chuckled. "You do have a point...not that you're the most companionable fairy. When you're writing, we don't see you for months, except for the complaints about too much noise and interruptions."

"Oh, please. Your snores alone are enough to keep the entire village awake. And when you try to sing—"

"Shut up, both of you." Rose fluffed her skirts in frustration. "Oh, dear, here they come."

Trumpets blared as the prince entered the list. He bowed to his mother and the ladies who sat beside her. But his expression could not be seen beneath the heavy visor he wore.

Graham entered next, a huge and menacing figure in his armor. But the heavy metal slowed him down, his usual quickness constrained by the massive weight he carried.

Snapdragon frowned. "His armor must be twice as heavy as the prince's."

"He's twice as big a man," Pansy replied, squinting against the metal's glare in the sun.

"He's not twice as big," Snapdragon huffed. "Well, maybe one and a half times as big," she added with a frown. "Are they really going to fight hand to hand? I thought this was supposed to be a joust."

Rose's lips thinned. "So did I. Graham certainly has a bit if a disadvantage on the ground. The prince's smaller size means he can move quicker."

"What did you expect, Rose?" Pansy shook her finger under the other fairy's nose. "That the prince would give Graham the upper hand?"

"We can't sit here and let them kill each other." Snapdragon rolled up her sleeve in determination, uncaring of the warning look Rose shot her.

The two men bowed briefly before coming together in a clank of metal and arms. Graham aimed high, but the prince parried and the strike slid harmlessly off the other man's shoulder. The prince stabbed straight toward Graham's gut. He hit his target and Graham doubled over, shaking his head as if to clear the shock away.

But he regrouped swiftly and rushed at the prince with his head lowered, like a raging bull charging into the fray. He would have knocked the prince on his royal ass, if he didn't suddenly stumble back as if he'd run into a thick brick wall.

"Did you see that?" Snapdragon squeaked excitedly. "He didn't even touch the prince. That's the best shell-spell I've ever done."

"Well, then, watch this." Pansy pointed to where the prince very slowly raised his sword in both hands. He moved as if through water, or as if he was at war with himself. "Slow-motion...a specialty of mine."

Rose snapped her fingers and a piece of glass appeared in her hands. She peered through her magnifying mirror for long breathless seconds. "Move his sword to the left, he's aiming straight for Graham's neck."

Snapdragon wiggled her fingers and the sword shook alarmingly in the prince's hands. "Damn, he is a strong one."

"Uh, oh," Rose said. "Graham's trying to roll out of the way. Better slow him down, too."

"Done." Pansy pointed and Graham slumped back against the ground. "This is fun," she added with a wicked delight. "I've wanted to put him in his place for days now."

ജ

"What the bloody hell?" Graham shook the fog from his brain. He felt like he'd just run into a mountain. His head pounded in the metal visor, and he was pinned to the ground by a force unlike anything he had ever felt before. No, he amended, choking on his rage. This reeked of fairy magic.

He would kill the three of them for good—if he actually managed to live through this, he added as he saw the prince standing over him with his sword ready to chop him off at the neck.

"Oh, shite," he swore as the blade dropped slowly toward

him. Did Bert really mean to kill him?

Then he saw the other man shake his head, as if he too was controlled by a force he could not fight, his arms trembling with the effort it took to keep the sword from moving...or so Graham desperately hoped.

"Can you hear me?" he shouted through his helmet, the words sounding muffled and faint.

The prince nodded. "I can't stop this," Graham thought he heard the man say.

"Hold on." Taking the chance of his life, Graham turned his head, trying to lift his hand enough to pull up the visor of his helmet. He hurriedly scanned the rows of spectators when he got a clear view of the field. There. He swore he saw three tiny slivers of light hovering over the booth where all three of their mothers sat.

"Come here, you miserable creatures," he bellowed. They would know just who he meant. A wave of relief washed over him when he saw them fly hesitantly towards them. And then he noticed something that made his blood run cold.

Earl Rulfert was no longer in the stands. Where had the man gone, and who was in danger now?

By the time they reached the two men, the fairies knew something was decidedly wrong. Graham's face was red with fury, but his expression was directed solely at them, not at the man still poised above him.

"Stop this now," Graham bit out.

The prince's arms were shaking so badly, Rose knew he couldn't hold out much longer. She whisked the sword from his hands and sent it spinning across the field. A roar from the crowd caused the fairies to jump in surprise.

"Don't worry," Snapdragon whispered, "they can't see us from here." She patted Graham's arm.

He jerked to his feet, smacking her away. "I saw you."

"Well, that's different." Pansy smoothed out her dress. "You were looking for us."

By now, Bert had removed his own helmet and gaped in shock at them.

Snapdragon snorted. "It is not polite to stare, no matter who you are."

"Don't ask," Graham said before the prince could form the question. "'Twould take too long to explain." He turned back to the stands. "Do you see who I don't see?"

The prince followed his gaze, his expression hardening. "No Rulfert." Then he paled. "Or Lila. You don't think he... I will personally flay the skin from his bones if he has harmed her in any way."

Snapdragon and Pansy puffed out their chests with pride. "We can find them," they stated, nearly in unison as they flew toward the castle.

Rose hesitated. Pansy and Snapdragon had always let their emotions get the better of them, making all the wrong decisions for all the right intentions. *A fairy's first duty was to carry out their assignment*—section one, subsection one, paragraph eleven of the charter. And in all her years of service, Rose had never once broken that sacred trust.

She turned back to the men in consternation, frightened, weak, and terribly alone.

Graham reached out to touch her shoulder. "Go on, Rose, Jiliana is at the castle. Keep her safe until I get there."

"With pleasure." She sighed in relief. "Hold on, you two," she added, flying fast behind the other two fairies. "I'm coming after all."

The earl dragged the weeping girl to the altar. Her hair shone like gold in the candle's light. "Here. Take her. She is perfect for what you need. Make the damn sacrifice and let's get on with it."

So beautiful, he thought as he slid the neko-te over his fingers one by one, admiring the sharpness of the lethal metal claws. He touched one to the girl's cheek and she screamed, the sound echoing off the walls like the sweet chime of temple bells.

"Please...stay. I will do my best to make certain you enjoy it." He bowed to the earl in respect, his face as calm as a new spring day. He had been given the perfect sacrifice, and the perfect way to follow tradition until the very end. "I will do you the greatest honor."

And then he struck, fast and hard, the neko-te tearing through skin and muscle in a single graceful move.

Chapter Fourteen

Jiliana slipped along the deserted hallway, her footsteps light as a feather come to rest. She paused at each open door to glance quickly inside, not even noticing the wealth displayed at every turn. Riches meant little if they served no higher purpose. The stone stairs were cold beneath her feet as she climbed to the second floor where glimmers of candlelight cast grotesque shadows that chased her upon the walls.

He was here. Waiting. Ready to kill unless she could stop him. Taking a deep breath, she caught a whiff of incense, the scent reminding her of courage and honor and the teachings of her masters.

The smell grew sharper, tendrils of smoke hanging ghostlike in the hall, still and lifeless, leading her toward a doorway just ahead. The chapel. Ironic that he had chosen this sacred place to perform the profanities of torture and murder.

She barely stirred the air as she entered the chamber to see a figure slumped on a bench near the altar. The stench of blood rose to mingle with the incense, turning the smell into a vile and nauseating brew. The figure didn't move as she worked her way down the aisle between rows of empty pews.

She held her *katana* at the ready as she stopped to examine the body. Earl Rulfert sat with his hands clasped over his stomach, his entrails spilling out between his fingers. His body had been ripped wide open, the claw marks of the leopard clear for her to see. To her horror, his eyes opened as she watched, he wasn't dead...at least not yet. Her brows knitted. This wasn't right. If the earl had hired the assassin, how could he have been the victim?

Something glittered on the floor, and Jiliana reached to pick up the familiar object...the earl's yellow diamond ring. Without thought, she tucked it into a pocket of her shirt before she left the man to die.

A gleam of gold caught her eye, and Jiliana felt her heart close tight as she rushed to kneel by the body on the floor. Her eyes stung with unshed tears as she brushed back a lock of Lila's hair, sticky and matted with blood from the knife wound in her stomach.

The girl moaned and tried to open her eyes.

"Shhhh," Jiliana soothed. "I am here." She could hear the emotion in her voice, its gruff sound not what she'd intended at all.

"I knew...you...would...come." Lila's voice faded to barely a whisper. She coughed, her spittle tinged red.

Jiliana cursed...pain and rage such as she'd thought forgotten rising hard to steal her breath as she remembered the sound of her father screaming at her to flee, his voice filled with anger and guilt. She finally understood what Graham had been trying to tell her.

Her father's rage had never been aimed at her...no more than her rage was now aimed at Lila. He had been as helpless then as Jiliana was now, unable to do more than watch and grieve as the scene played out to its awful truth.

Lila's breath began to fail but she managed to reach out and touch Jiliana's cheek, the gesture soft and final. "Your...friend," she said on a sigh, her hand dropping lifeless to the floor.

Jiliana's life had come full circle, and the sorrow threatened to tear her in two. She couldn't move, she couldn't think, the overwhelming grief more than she could manage.

There was no meaning to this death.

The chapel door slammed shut and Jiliana froze, forcing her mind to lock the pain away. It lodged bitter in her soul, adding its weight to the already massive void. A whisper of ice slithered over her heart, the briefest hint of the freeze that was to come. She stood to face the figure that came toward her from the shadows, her brutal smile hiding all her pain.

"I did not kill the girl," he said, walking calmly down the aisle. "You must believe me." Again, her confusion mounted. This man was not from the east. The cadence of his voice marked him as being from Westmyre.

"Who are you?" Her *katana* lifted as if it had life of its own, pointing steady and strong at the man's throat. Step by step, she moved toward him, every muscle tensing in anticipation as she approached.

Almost...she was almost near enough to strike when she caught a glimpse of his face.

"*Chikuso!*" Jiliana jumped back as she recognized Reginald, the earl's nephew. "You." She let her sword drop to show she was not a threat. ""I am not here to hurt you, my lord. Are you injured?"

"No." He shook his head. "I am quite well." His hand rested casually on the hilt of his sword—his right hand, she noted quickly. "But how did you get here? I had heard you were arrested and locked way." His fingers curled around his sword-hilt. "There must be a price on your head by now."

"Listen to me." She had to take control of the situation before he did anything stupid. "I am here on the prince's order.

Your uncle was suspected of treason, and I was sent to find the proof." Her eyes narrowed. "Since you don't seem to be involved in any way, I suggest you go find the prince and Sir Graham and tell them what has happened, before you put your own life in danger."

Dismissing him, Jiliana turned to scan the rest of the chapel, her gaze searching out every possible hiding place, her ears attuned to any possible sound. Nothing, yet the ice continued to swirl along her veins, its familiar chill warning her of danger.

She turned back to find Reginald two steps closer, his face calm and completely composed. She hadn't heard his boots make a sound on the floor...unnatural, especially for a man of the west.

The ice crept further into her chest.

Nevertheless, she gave him a friendly smile while she reached into her pocket. "Your uncle's ring," she said, tossing it casually toward him.

Reflexively, he reached out to catch it...with his left hand. A single hiss of pain left his lips, but it was enough. It all fell into place as he bared his teeth and drew his sword—a *katana*, its blade a foot longer than her own.

"Your uncle never did step foot out of Westmyre." Jiliana flicked her wrist, bringing her own *katana* back up. "But you did."

"Jiliana-san." He bent his head in a subtle bow. "I spent many years learning the way of the warrior. Such total dedication to their art. Such precision of their craft." His eyes half-closed in rapture. "Such beauty."

"And brutality." Her lips twisted as she mocked him.

He laughed, the hollow sound echoing off the cold stone walls. "I heard of you during my stay in the Secret City. You are

197

called *she-who-slaughters*, and your name is spoken of in wonder. There are many who would kill to know the secret of your talent."

His words had the desired effect. Her guilt rose, painful and raw. "Talent? I would not call it that." Jiliana nodded at his arm. "I hit too low yesterday. I was not expecting a man of the west. Is it healing well?"

She was deliberately drawing his attention to the injury. Although he hid the pain well, she knew it must be agonizing. He would guard that arm more closely than the rest of his body. When instinct warred with discipline, the warrior fought two battles, and his focus was distracted accordingly. Her lips turned up in contempt. "You were slow, a mistake a master never would have made."

He lunged without warning, his blade flying through the air as if it were made of nothing more than wind. She parried with a strike of her own, their swords meeting with an ear-splitting clash. But Reginald was strong enough to take the blow, and when Jiliana faltered, he drove her back, driving a spear-hand into her stomach. She retched as the blow sank home, his fingers bruising muscle and organs.

He stepped back and studied her pleasantly. "It is healing excellently." Reginald laid his *katana* negligently over his shoulder.

Arrogant, she thought, struggling to catch her breath. It was a weakness she could use. If she could keep him feeling like he was the one in control, it would give her a chance to study him...even for a few moments.

As if they were discussing nothing more than the weather, Jiliana asked, "Why did you kill your uncle? Did you want more money and he refused?"

When his expression darkened, she knew she struck a

nerve. "This was never about the money...how dare you insult me that way." He pointed his *katana* at her in accusation, his face growing flushed with the force of his emotion.

"Forgive me." Never letting her gaze leave his face, she bowed slightly. "I should have known better. Was he backing out? Could he not stomach the necessary deaths?"

Reginald shook his head violently. "On the contrary. He was wasteful...unmindful of the proper way. He never understood the sacrifices. He never saw the beauty." A sneer turned up his lip. "He was without honor."

Jiliana nodded, pretending she was in total agreement. "They are like beasts, these men of Westmyre. Men playing stupidly at war." She remembered the earl had used that same phrase.

Reginald's face grew rapturous. "I knew you would understand, Jiliana-san. And that is why I waited for you to come."

His tongue flicked out to lick his lips. She watched the gesture through disdainful eyes. For all his talk of honor and tradition, he had yet to master the basics of battle, unable to even control his own actions.

"I can give you a gift beyond price," he continued, sweat beading his upper lip. "The chance to offer your life in exchange for the one you serve."

Jiliana shuddered at the thought, a flicker of fear trailing up her spine. To die in battle was one thing. To make herself a sacrifice was another matter entirely. Did he really think she would agree to his madness?

"I could just kill you instead," she stated, shifting her weight as she readied to attack. "And still do my duty to the crown."

All emotion bled from his face, his eyes turning cold and

void of compassion. For an instant she saw his true nature...a twisted thing as dangerous as the monster hiding in her heart.

"I will send my prayers, *kono-yaro*—you bastard," she said, without a glimmer of remorse, "when I release your spirit to the ancestors."

"*Hail*" With a yell, Jiliana leapt in for the strike, pivoting at the very last minute to slice at his leg instead. He blocked the blow and grinned, countering with a kick to her shoulder. She slid out of the way easily, landing an elbow to his ribs as she ducked beneath the sword that sliced through air where her neck had been.

Rolling on the ground, Jiliana struck his calf as she passed, knowing by his grunt of pain that she managed to draw first blood. But she controlled her emotions. Although Reginald's arrogance had saved her life before, she doubted even he was foolish enough to give her a second chance.

He swung and missed, spinning completely around to stab at her from behind. Jiliana side-stepped, her reflexes taking over. Out of the corner of her eye she saw Lila's crumpled form. She felt her monster rear its head, but for once she welcomed it with open arms. He would pay for her life, and those of the others he'd murdered without cause. It was the law...and she was the executioner.

The world faded, growing grey and insubstantial in the back of her mind. On some level she knew that many came to watch, ghostlike figures that sped past her vision, formless specters from a completely different realm. She ignored them all, even Graham's familiar presence.

She and her enemy moved too fast for an outsider to interfere. For long moments they flowed together and apart in the deadly dance of battle, their bodies moving with little conscious thought, reacting and adjusting to each strike and counter-strike in an ancient rhythm born in blood.

Either she would kill Reginald or meet her death on the edge of his blade. No one else could change her fate now.

Sweat pooled beneath his arms and his face grew pale. A trail of blood stained the sleeve of his shirt as the wound burst open from the force of their intent. Good. He was starting to wear down.

Their *katanas* met, parted and met again, sparks flickering off the metal like fireflies at night. Jiliana barely felt the slice that bit into her thigh, but she knew it damaged muscle when her leg refused to bear her weight.

She heard the onlookers gasp as she fell at his feet, Graham's curse louder than the rest. Reginald, letting his ego take control once more, bowed mockingly, straddling her body as he raised his weapon high.

"Give my respect to your uncle," she told him, both hands glued to the hilt of her sword. Swinging up with every bit of strength she had, she sliced through his waist as he bent to finish her off.

The disbelief on his face was a joy for her to watch as her *katana* bit through skin and muscle and bone, severing his body completely in two.

He toppled over slowly, his expression still incredulous, even in death.

Graham watched in horrid fascination as Jili sliced through Reginald Blenham's body as easily as a butcher cutting through a side of beef. Because she still wore her mask, he couldn't read any expression on her face. But the way she moved...the way she held her *katana*...the way she turned to face the crowd, all told him that this could explode into an even more dangerous situation.

She melted into a shadowy corner of the room as Bert bent over the upper half of the body and bared the left shoulder. A long gash had been roughly sewn together. "It bears out her story...that she injured him in the stable. Do you think she knew he was our assassin?"

Graham shook his head, keeping Jili always at the edge of his vision. "I don't know." He jerked his chin at the body of the earl, the grisly sight more worthy of a charnel house than the chapel of the castle. "Looks like Rulfert was a last sacrifice." Jili scooted closer and his gaze raced to follow her every move. He nodded when the prince looked his way, assuring the man he knew there would be trouble. "Get out. All of you, now."

Bert motioned his men to leave, stopping to speak to Graham on his way out the door. "Be careful, brother, she is not the woman you know."

No. She wasn't, he realized when they were alone and she gave no sign of recognition. Graham shuddered.

Battle-shock.

He had only seen this one other time before, during the war to restore Edgar to the throne. A man had gone berserk, unable to stop killing long after the day had been won. Eventually he turned on his friends and companions. They couldn't stop him. He was put down like a rabid dog, eight arrows shot into his neck and chest before he finally succumbed to a bloody death.

How could he face that with Jili? His gut clenched as she took a step toward him, the flash of metal all the warning he had before the iron star hit his cheek, splitting the skin and scraping into bone. Blood spurted into his eyes and he barely saw Jili run to the body to take a second sword in her hand.

"Jili, 'tis me, Graham." He refused to be swayed by the pain. She didn't know what she was doing. He put all his love into his voice, hoping somehow that she might hear it through her madness. "The battle is over. You won. Put down your sword and we can go home."

The mask obliterated everything from her expression. He had no way of knowing if she heard him or not...no way to judge her eyes in the shadows. He had to get closer. And the only way he could do that was by drawing his own sword. "Jili...Jili, listen to me."

She cocked her head as if she might have heard, hesitating long enough for him to pull out his blade. He held it relaxed at his side. If she lunged he could parry. He had learned enough about her style of fighting to know how and when she would attack.

The problem was she knew everything about his style, also. And in her present state, she would not have the same qualms about hurting him as he did about injuring her. It put him at a decided disadvantage. It was a weakness he couldn't afford. "Finella and Sam—"

She attacked before he could finish the thought, one sword hitting high and left, the other stabbing straight to his stomach. He took a huge step toward her, coming in closer than she'd expected. He parried the strike to his stomach with his own blade, blocking the other with his arm, trying to grab her wrist before she could aim again.

He missed. Her *katana* sliced through the back of his wrist to the bone. He cursed, but gave no more thought to the injury. It wasn't deadly, not by any means.

She had already re-grouped, spinning around to slice at his back. He dropped in a practiced move, hitting her hard on the thigh with the flat side of his broadsword. Despite the force of the blow, she did not go down, and only the quilting of his gambeson kept the swords from doing more damage than a scratch.

"Jili, stop!" Graham tried again to get through her detachment, wrapping his arms around her legs before she could come at him again, throwing her to the floor hard enough to make her moan.

He pinned her with his weight, one hand slamming hers to the ground, over and over until she let go of the weapon. He threw it across the room when she reached for it again.

"One down, one to go," he said, gritting his teeth when she dug one finger into the hollow of his throat, the force enough to make him gag. When this was over, he planned on having her teach him that trick, along with several others...like the way she managed to free one knee and jerk it into his groin. Sloppy but effective, causing him to choke again. "Shite! Woman, this is not funny at all."

Again, that briefest of hesitations as if she was trying to understand. But as he watched her raise her other sword to slice off one of his ears, Graham realized there was only one thing he could do. "Forgive me, love," he whispered before he rammed one massive fist into her jaw.

Her head hit the floor with a sickly thud, but the blow had the desired effect. She lay still and motionless beneath him, her fingers releasing the sword at last.

After pulling the mask from her face, he checked to make certain he hadn't done any serious damage. Her cheeks were pale, but her breath was stable. No blood matted her hair, and although she would have quite a bruise on her cheek, he didn't think he had actually broken bone.

After wrapping his own wrist to stop the bleeding, he picked her up and held her hard to his chest.

The fairies flew slowly from their vantage point, their faces stark and white. They hadn't been able to do a thing but watch as the battle played out beneath them. They could not be certain their spells would work in time, as swiftly as Jiliana and the other man had moved. Unused to being so helpless, their confidence had taken a dreadful blow.

Even now, as Graham picked up Jiliana and carried her from the chapel, there was nothing for them to do...until Rose spotted the girl lying near the altar.

"Is she dead?" Snapdragon hovered at her mouth, feeling for any sign of breath.

Pansy shook her head, refusing to go near them. "If she isn't she will be soon. It's too late."

Snapdragon shook her head. "Not yet." But her eyes were solemn as she glanced at her friends. "It will take a lot of magic to save her."

Rose nodded, her own expression bleak. "I know, dear."

"We won't be able to go home," Pansy added, finally moving to join the others, her spirits sinking fast. "Not for a very long time."

Chapter Fifteen

Jiliana woke up slowly. She felt as if she'd been run over by a herd of horses, and every muscle screamed in protest as she lifted her head to scan the room.

A panic rose in her chest as she realized she was still in the castle. It was evening...or dawn. The pale light from the window could have been either. Through the fog that clouded her wits, she couldn't remember whether she had bested Reginald or not.

She rolled off the bed, biting her lip against the pain as she landed on the cold stone floor, her hands already searching for anything she could use as a weapon. Footsteps. She listened intently as they came closer. Somehow she managed to crawl to the door and stand shaking beside it, waiting to pounce on whoever came in. It squeaked alarmingly as it opened, giving her the cover she needed. She jumped the moment the man stepped into the room, her arms curling in a death grip around his throat.

"Damn it, Jili." Graham roared in frustration, dropping the tray he carried as he tried to pull her fingers free. "That was a bowl of the best vegetable soup Samantha has ever made."

"Graham." The rush of relief was followed just as quickly by a rush of horrid shame. "It happened, didn't it?" She let him go to slump against the wall, her memories struggling to surface. She swallowed against the nausea that threatened to choke her.

Stepping over the mess she'd made, Graham swept her into his arms and carried her back to bed. "You killed Reginald. Bert is fine, and the queen is determined to knight you at the first possible opportunity." His tone was practiced and steady, giving nothing of his emotions away.

She killed Reginald. She killed him. She killed him. "*Kuso*," she muttered as the images began to form. The swing of her *katana*...the deadly concentration...the strike...the blood. She closed her eyes, hoping to force the picture away, but it remained strong in her mind, Reginald's body severed at the waist, his top half sliding to the floor while his legs still tried take a step.

"I cut him in two." Her voice betrayed her horror. "How could I have done that? I'm not strong enough for such a—" She looked at Graham, searching his face for the truth. "You saw."

"Yes."

She was grateful he didn't deny it. A lie would have broken her spirit completely.

"Lila." Grief lodged like a solid weight in her chest. "She's—"

"Waiting to see you," Graham interjected. He smiled at her bemused expression. "The fairy-queens pulled off a miracle."

Her relief was swift and welcome. At least the girl hadn't paid a price to be her friend.

Graham let her go and pulled away. A cold crept over her and she began to shiver, but she did not ask him to hold her again. She didn't deserve the comfort, monster that she was. "Tell me." His expression dared her to the truth. She owed him that much, she realized, regardless of what would happen in the future.

"I could never let go of the night of the fire. The masters warned me time and again that my anger would rise up and destroy me, but I didn't listen. And every time I was hurt or humiliated or punished, I tucked those emotions away with my past, adding them to the layers of pain I forged to protect me. If I got to the point where I couldn't feel, I reasoned, I would become invincible...a warrior worthy of whoever commanded me. I used detachment as a way to advance." She broke off when a soft knock sounded at the door.

"Oh, my dears," came Lady Samantha's soft voice. "I had hoped..." She held up a candle against the gloom, her face a mask of concern when she saw the food splattered on the floor.

"'Tis alright, Mother," Graham assured. "Mayhaps you would leave the candle and bring another tray?"

He stood and moved to grab the light, giving his mother a hug before she smiled and left again. In the glow, Jiliana finally got a good look at his face, his cheek swollen to twice its size, a nasty gash running from the edge of his eye to the corner of his mouth.

"What happened?" she demanded, although she knew the answer. "I did that. I attacked you."

He sighed and sat down on the bed, touching a finger to her jaw. She winced and he frowned. "And I did that." He tried to smile, biting back a groan when the stitches pulled too tight. "I am sorry I had to hurt you."

"I'm not. You would have had to kill me otherwise." She regretted the words as soon as she saw his haunted expression. "Graham, I don't blame you for anything, and I wouldn't have blamed you if—"

"Don't you dare say that. Not ever." He ran his hand through his hair and looked anywhere but at her. "I refuse to think of how close I came to losing you."

She reached out and took his chin in her hand, forcing him to face her. "I can't stay, Graham, not now. I can't control myself. How could I claim to love you when I put you in danger every day of your life? How could you ever sleep wondering if the next fight we had would turn me back into a killer?"

"Jili, it wasn't like that." But this time she saw the lie he tried to hide. And while she hated him for it, she hated herself even more.

"Get out. Just get the hell out and leave me alone. You can't save me—haven't you figured that out by now?"

"Can we come in?" They both turned to see Finella and Samantha standing in the door with more candles and a fresh tray of food.

"Graham, we would very much like to speak with Jiliana...alone." Finella strode purposefully across the floor. "Your brothers are waiting for you downstairs." She frowned. "They have brought up an entire barrel of Rulfert's best ale."

When he hesitated, Jiliana knew he was waiting for her to ask him to stay. Instead, she turned her face into the pillow, hearing him kiss his mothers before closing the door behind him.

Not that she felt comforted by having to face the two women and explain herself all over again. They sat on the edge of the bed, watching her through sorrowful eyes.

Lady Samantha was the first to speak. She took Jiliana's hand and leaned in close to tuck her matted hair behind one ear. "Did we do wrong, Jiliana, to send you away all those years ago?" Her voice was sad, quiet, and earnest. "Maybe we should have kept you here with us, and given you more time to heal."

"No." Jiliana shook her head. "You did everything I asked. It was my fault alone that I could not let go of my anger. Now it is too late, and I have only myself to blame." Her eyes filled with unexpected tears. She fought them back as she always did.

Finella spoke next. "Graham loves you. He would do

anything in his power to protect you." She smoothed Jiliana's shirt and busied herself plumping the pillows. "He is a man of his word."

She struggled to sit higher, disentangling herself from their ministrations. "You don't understand. I am not the one needing protection. If I stay, I put everyone here at risk. Did you see what I am capable of?" Both women paled. "That could be Graham next...or one of you...or one of the children. I am not worth any of that."

"Of course you are, dear." Finella snorted. "Us Dunmore women are worthy of everything."

It surprised her to realize how much she adored these two ladies, how much she had relished their letters over the years, and how much she had looked forward to coming home and seeing them again. But her lips refused to form the words. Regret and longing speared a path into her heart. So many things waiting just beyond her reach. So much of a different life taunting her from the distance.

Samantha smiled, shedding the tears that Jiliana still could not. "No matter what you say, we will never forgive ourselves for letting you go away. We made that mistake once before, with the boys' father, and should have known better than to do it again."

When she reached to hug her, Jiliana stiffened and pulled away. In all her life she had rarely known a mother's touch, and it threatened to overwhelm her as the child in her raced to be comforted.

But she was no longer a child. She was no longer even capable of rediscovering that part of her spirit. "I thank you both again," she said stiffly, turning back upon herself as she always did. "I will forever be grateful for your many kindnesses."

Finella gave her a sterner glance. "Our kindnesses will not

stop here, girl, no matter what you decide or where you are." She stood and held out her hand for Samantha. "Come. She is tired. We have done our best...for now."

"Goodnight, Jiliana," Samantha said, placing a kiss on her cheek just the same. "If you need anything, just call."

In a practiced discipline, Jiliana forced herself to eat. She would need all her strength to pack and leave.

ജ

"You don't have to do this." Graham stood in the doorway, his arms folded across his chest.

Although her heart was breaking, Jiliana refused to let him see. Better a clean good-bye than to cling and weep like some fool in the throes of her first true love—even if the description fit. She stuffed a spare shirt and *hakama* in a bag and tossed it over her shoulder. Her *katana* hung by her side as always, its presence both a boon and a bane. She did not know if she could ever use it again, but it would certainly prove an impressive threat if anyone chose to confront her.

Graham watched through lidded eyes, his presence making her decision that much harder. "Where will you go?"

She shrugged, avoiding his gaze, a cowardly gesture at best. "I have enough money to go wherever I want. Maybe south...maybe north."

To her consternation, he stepped farther into the room, closing the door behind him. She heard the lock turn with decided dread. Jiliana clenched her jaw, anger rising swiftly to the surface. She was too bruised, too vulnerable to put up with any nonsense from him now. Her emotions had refused to settle at all these past two days, and she knew she needed to get away before they spun out of control and did any more damage. "Get out of my way. You know as well as I do this is the only option I have."

"No." His voice was as bleak as his expression. He leaned against the door as if daring her to move him. "I don't know this is the only option. I think you're just too much of a coward to stay and face what you've done." When one hand dropped to her *katana* before she could stop the gesture, he noticed and gave her a mocking smile. "You can't do a damned thing without it, can you?" He gestured at the weapon. "You use it like a wedge to keep anyone from getting near."

"So what?" She jutted up her chin. "It doesn't have a thing to do with you. 'Tis my life to live as I see fit. Now get the hell out of my way."

"Make me." He crooked his finger, the come hither motion a definite challenge. "But before you do, put the *katana* down. See if you can take me one on one."

She gaped at him, wondering at his sheer stupidity. "You don't get it do you? I can't stay. What happens the next time I lose control? What if I hurt someone...you...one of your family...one of the children? I can't be trusted."

For the first time she heard the pain that underscored her words, and knew he heard it, too. No matter...she didn't care if he pitied her. It was far too late for such futile pride. "I almost killed you, Graham. Have you forgotten that already?"

He stubbornly shook his head. "That's not how I saw it."

As the scene replayed itself in her mind, her fury rose another notch, bolstered by the fear of what she had almost done, and what she could very well do again. Why couldn't he get that through his thick addled skull? "You are a stupid ass who doesn't know shite about shite!"

He laughed, the sound rolling across the room, making her

feel like she was the idiot, and he was the one in the right of things. "Prove it. Take off your sword and try and take me down. If you can, you walk away, no questions asked, and I won't stop you."

"And if I don't?"

"Then you stay here, become my wife, and we live happily ever after." For an instant she saw the sorrow that he tried hard to hide. They had been close, she realized, her own pain struggling to choke her, so close to having the kind of life she had never even dreamed of.

But it was not meant to be. And the sooner he realized the awful truth of her the better. With resignation, she sat her bag on the floor and unbuckled her sword-belt. Her hands trembled as she handed Graham the blade.

As she watched in complete surprise, he moved to the window and tossed her beautiful weapon out like a pile of refuse from the garbage. The bastard. She had earned that sword...put her life on the line to earn it. How dare he treat it with such disrespect?

She took a step toward him, hands already raised in position, but before she had a chance to strike, Graham elbowed her in the chest, not even turning from where he gazed out the window. The blow knocked her on her ass, forcing the air from her lungs to leave her gasping like a dying fish on the floor, struggling to regain her breath.

He turned to watch her with a smile on his beautiful treacherous face, his head cocked as if he was studying some slimy creature crawled out from the gutter. "I think I won that round," he said, stepping from the window to glare down at her. "Care for round two?"

In response, Jiliana kicked at his ankle, intending to knock his leg out from under him, but he had learned that particular trick. Side-stepping quickly, he grabbed her foot and twisted, forcing her onto her stomach as she screamed in pain and impotence.

"Hmmmmm, round two seems to have gone my way, as well." When she rolled over to face him, he raised an eyebrow in amusement. "This is going much easier than I thought. Where shall we hold the wedding? Llew wants us to come to Dunmore Keep, but I would prefer—"

"*Hai!*" She kicked high this time, catching him fully in the groin. He choked, his face turning purple as he doubled over in pain. "What were you saying, dear?" She did a front roll and sprang easily to her feet, backhanding him in the stomach. It was her turn to smile as he fell to his knees.

Her rage was a living thing. Hot. Wild. Flaming out of control. And she reveled in every second of the madness.

She prowled closer, looking for her opening, bringing her knee up hard and fast...but Graham caught her just before she connected with his chin, wrapping his hands around her knee and throwing her across the chamber. She hit the wall with a solid thud, fury making her speechless.

"—to have the wedding here," Graham continued as if he'd never been interrupted. He rose to his feet and walked toward her, the look on his face almost enough to make her tremble. "I think this fall would be nice, or would you like a winter wedding?"

Although she aimed a punch at his cheek, he turned his head too fast and she ended up ramming her fingers against the too solid muscle of his shoulder. Jiliana grunted as the pain radiated all the way up her arm.

That really hurt, she thought in wonder, barely blocking his palm-strike to her ribs. But she was too slow to block his other hand. He pounded her solidly on the jaw, and she tasted blood as she bit into her cheek.

"*Baka*," she mouthed, barreling into his chest. Ridge-hand. Palm-strike. Knife-hand. Knee. Neck, chest, stomach and groin.

"Shite, woman, do you want to have children or not?" She thought his bellow could be heard for miles around. She knew it when she heard the laughter coming from the other side of the door.

"Are they all out there?" she demanded.

"Only Llew and Allard," he answered with a squeak. "Bert and Wynn are discussing a new road system for the northern marshes." Despite his seeming incapacitation, he charged at her in a second, grabbing a handful of her hair, and ramming her into the wall once more. "Or summer, if you don't mind a simple ceremony." His breath fanned her cheek, hot and tempting against her skin.

She struggled, bit, tried to kick and failed, all the while assuring him in no uncertain terms that she would never...ever...not in a million years...

And then it hit her, so fast her knees went weak. She was mad, yes. Furious, yes. Ready to make him beg for mercy—but she was not losing control. She felt it still...lurking in her darkness, but for now, at least, it had no reason to resurface.

Graham held back the fist he'd cocked, watching the joy race across her face. "Thank God," he muttered as he slid down the wall to the floor, pulling her with him. She let him sit her on his lap and tuck her head beneath his chin. "Tell me the rest of it. I'm not stupid, Jili," he added when she peeked up at him. "I know there's more to your story."

She put her hand over his heart, feeling the strong and steady beat. "It isn't pretty."

"Doesn't have to be. It just has to be the truth." He kissed her head and wrapped his arms around her. "I love you.

Nothing will ever change that. I promise."

She had to smile. Graham never made a promise he didn't keep. His honor was without question. "Can we at least get some wine? I could use something to dull the pain."

Graham grunted when she shifted her weight on his lap. "So could I. Llew, Allard," he yelled at the door, "one of you fools get us something to drink. And don't worry, she isn't going to kill me."

Laughter from the hall. "We were worried about you, little brother," came a friendly voice. "We knew you had finally met your match."

"So I have," he answered. When he tugged a lock of her hair she snuggled closer, causing him to groan again. "I swear, woman, as much as I cannot resist you, I doubt I could properly bed you tonight. In the future, you will not bust my balls on a daily basis."

They heard bottles set on the floor, followed by a knock and footsteps fading down the hallway.

"Our wine." He tried to stand, but she pushed him back, frowning when he winced.

"I'll get it."

He nodded. "Good idea."

She meant to sit next to him after she'd retrieved the bottles, but he pulled her back on his lap, grunting only once when her bottom landed between his legs. His brothers had already opened the wine, and she took a drink before handing it over.

Graham took a very long swallow. "Mmmmm, Rulfert had good taste. Go on," he prodded with a contented sigh.

Although she didn't think she would know where to start, Jiliana found the words fell easily from her tongue, as if she had been waiting years for this very moment. "The first time was at the school. We had a new student. His family couldn't control him and he was sent to learn discipline. Just as we were about to spar, he told me I was weak...a stupid outsider who had no business in their land. He said he planned to sneak into my chamber that night and...well, you know." She reached for the bottle.

"He scared you."

"He terrified me," she admitted. "All I could think of was how horrible it had been, and that I would never let it happen to me again. I don't remember anything else until they pulled us apart. He was cut in a dozen places. The masters warned me that if I couldn't control my pain and guilt, I would not be allowed to study the sword."

"So you did control it...at first." Graham picked up a second bottle and grinned. It ended in a grimace when his stitches pulled too tight. "I must look like a monster," he said.

Jiliana reached up to touch his cheek. "You are still the most beautiful man I have ever seen. I am so very sorry," she added in a whisper.

In answer he kissed her, the softest of touches. "I was far too pretty before. This way, my brothers won't feel so horribly ugly."

She tried to laugh, but the sound was tempered by sadness. Even if he never admitted to the loss, Jiliana knew the damage she had caused. It would take a very long time for her to forgive herself.

"I did manage to control myself," she continued, forcing this new guilt aside. "Not completely, like they thought. I could feel it...this hole...a void that was always waiting. Because I was a woman, I was sent to guard the emperor's daughters. I learned things there I shouldn't have..." She let her voice trail off.

"Don't you dare stop now," he ordered. "Have another drink, 'twill loosen your lovely tongue." He gave her a naughty wink. "Not that I need it today," he finished when he straightened one leg and the muscle cramped. "Hellfire!" he swore, jumping when her hands dug into the knotted muscle.

"Better?" She pressed her fingers hard into his thigh, and the muscle slowly relaxed once again.

"Quit changing the subject."

"I wasn't."

"You were."

Her temper flared briefly, hot and alive. Jiliana smiled into his chest, enjoying the sensible emotion. "One day one of the princesses wanted to go for a walk. I was stupid and let her talk me into going off the palace grounds. We were attacked. When it was over, and I saw what I had done...I knew what had happened. Six men nearly ripped to shreds. I should have left that very day, but when the emperor gave me the *katana*—" She raised her head and looked him directly in the eye. "It was the only thing I had ever earned...the only thing I could truly claim was mine. Does that make any stupid sense?"

"As much as any stupid reason. I know what 'tis like, Jili, to need something to be proud of. And I have never been alone like you have." His eyes darkened and his voice grew rough. "Not that I will ever let you go. I'm bigger than you are, and you'd better not forget it."

"I cannot keep it." The certainty that washed over her put her heart at peace. She could stay, but she could not keep the blade. It would be her sacrifice, her promise for their future. And as she understood the price, she felt a part of herself let go, a layer of her pain and sorrow peel away to catch the wind. It would not happen overnight, but in the security of Graham's love she would someday heal. It was a beginning. It was more than enough.

"Do you know how much I love you, *baka*?" Her heart felt as open as the sky. "I have loved you all my life, since that very first day you listened to my secrets." She welcomed the sting of tears, and for once made no effort to hide them. "I didn't know then I would have so very many."

"I think this would be a good time to stop," Graham replied, running a hand across her breast. "Unless, of course, you want to whisper some wicked secret in my ear."

Jiliana grinned and reached for the wine, enjoying the warmth of it in her stomach. He might be a fool, but he was her fool, and she loved every joke he tried to make. "I have another tattoo," she said, laughing in delight when he choked on his drink and spewed wine across the room.

Without warning the prince pushed open the door and poked his head in. "It sounded safe. You two look like hell," he said with a grimace. "Remind me to marry a woman who can barely lift my cock."

Graham snorted, his lip curling in derision. "You're too soft. What happens the next time we're not there to save your sorry ass?"

Bertram—Egbert, Jiliana corrected—sat on the edge of the bed and smiled. "About that." He cleared his throat. "It seems I have an opening for captain of the royal guard, Duncemore. You get the job."

"Whether I like it or not?" Graham's voice was amused. "What if I say no...you going to threaten to chop off my head again? Imprison me for insubordination? Oh, no, brother, we are far beyond such petty squabbles."

As Jiliana watched the prince's mouth thin, she took another drink of wine. They were likely to argue all night, and if she had to listen, she might as well be drunk enough not to mind.

"'Tis no petty argument, you addle-brained pig." Egbert reached for the bottle. She handed it over without a word. "I am giving you a position most men would beg for."

Graham laughed, the sound ending in a cough when his chest muscles spasmed. "I am not most men."

"Agreed." The prince's eyes sharpened. "What would it take to make you say yes...just out of curiosity." Although his expression remained sober, Jiliana could see the humor hovering just below the surface. The two might bicker like children, but they loved every minute of it.

"What do you think, Jili?" Graham gave her a wink. "Should we go and whip his men into some semblance of a royal guard? If he is going to be king, I guess he should live long enough to enjoy it."

Jiliana pretended to frown. "Isn't there some rule that states the crown can only be guarded by a lord...or higher? That lets you off the hook, my love."

Graham slapped his thigh, wincing when he hit a bruise. "She makes a good point." He reached out and the wine exchanged hands once more. "And we should talk about pay. I am worth my weight in gold."

Now it was the prince's turn to laugh. "Half your bloody weight," he corrected. "I will not pay for the excess flab you mistakenly call muscle."

"Care to test that theory, my friend?" Graham's tone darkened as he tried to stand, only to fall back to the floor with a bellow that could be heard for miles around. "Tomorrow," he added with a grimace. "Or mayhaps the day after that...next week certainly at the latest."

"Half your weight in gold...Rulfert's title and estate."

Egbert's voice held a practiced negligence that didn't fool anyone. He was desperate to have Graham accept the position. "And I promise not to cut off your head despite the fact you show me no respect whatsoever."

"And Lila," Jiliana intervened. Both men stared at her in varying degrees of surprise, the prince's being the greatest of the two.

Graham's grin grew as the prince's smile faltered. "And Lila," he echoed in true delight.

Jiliana elbowed him in the stomach. "Not for what you think, *baka*," she assured him primly. "She will be under my care at all times." She raised a brow in the prince's direction. "So, do we have an agreement?"

"Your lady seems to have taken lessons from our mothers." He shook his head at Graham. "You should stop this behavior now before you live to regret it."

"'Tis too damned late," Graham said, sighing heavily. "I am cursed with a woman who thinks she is as good as any man." He tugged a lock of her hair and smiled. "Truth be told, I think she is right."

"Then I wish you the best of luck." Egbert leaned forward and held out his hand. "We are agreed, then...brother?"

Graham copied the gesture. "Oh yes, Bert. When do I need to be at the palace to kick your royal ass into shape?"

"Two weeks? Surely your horn will have worn out by then."

Graham traced a finger down Jiliana's cheek. "I don't think you should bet on that."

Prince Egbert grunted as he headed for the door. "Three weeks then, but 'tis my final offer."

Chapter Sixteen

Graham spun her around and cupped both Jiliana's breasts in his hands, the skin to skin contact causing her to tremble like smoke in the wind.

He had huge strong hands that made her feel small and feminine despite the fact she stood a head taller than most other women she'd ever met. In her years at Kyomo, she'd learned to use her size to her advantage, but as a woman she'd always felt an ogre next to the tiny and dainty women of the east.

Graham had changed all that. In his arms she could be supple and slim, a twig to his trunk...a stream to his river.

He growled, his fingers plucking at her nipples until she cried out in answer. "Very good," he whispered, the words like silk against her ear. "Our lesson for tonight, submission to your master."

When she opened her mouth to tell him that he was most certainly not her master, he let her go. "Say it, Jili," he demanded, refusing to touch her. "We both know who will win this night."

Her rational mind ordered her to refuse, but her body begged her to comply. And she was tired of fighting...tired of trying to stay in control. It was time to submit, to let go and find her bliss in his arms.

"Master." She finally managed to say the word, much as she knew he would never let her forget it. But it didn't matter when he pulled her back to his chest. The heat of his skin burned against hers, the intimacy fierce and heady. In the time it took for a raindrop to fall, he untied the sash of her *hakama,* letting the pants fall to a heap at her feet.

She felt wild and free in the hot summer night, the empress granting her favors to the warrior she'd chosen. Graham slid a hand across her stomach to brush the triangle of hair at its base, the touch setting her world alight.

"Tell your master, how you like your pleasure." He took her nipples in his fingers, pinching them just the smallest bit. "More or less?" He made no move to change the pressure, waiting for her answer.

Jiliana squirmed as need overtook her, her hunger stronger than her indecision. "More," she begged arching into his hands. He increased the pressure and waited once again.

It still was not enough. Why was he treating her like some porcelain doll, so fragile it had to be kept on a shelf? "More...master," she said, sucking in her breath when his fingers tightened around her pebbled flesh. "Ummmmm." Her nipples burned where he pinched them, the pain adding a deeper edge to her desire. She wanted it, she realized, wanted the darkness to overtake them both. She fought against him as he drew his hands away, his rumble of laughter adding weight to her frustration.

When she turned to aim a knee at his stomach, he grabbed her leg and wrapped it around his waist instead. The mass of his cock pressed between her thighs, insistent, impatient, daunting in its size.

She imagined his jade scepter burrowing inside her, hot and hard as it breached her gate of jewels. She shuddered at the thought...but not in fear. She kept her leg curled around him as he slid his hand along the inside of her thigh. His other hand grabbed a hunk of her hair, forcing her face up to his.

"More or less?" he asked again, his mouth not yet touching hers.

He was going to kill her if he didn't stop this insanity. Less? How could he give her any less? She took his hand and pressed it between her legs, clenching her teeth when he did nothing but rub his thumb gently over her clit.

"Please...more," she found herself begging against his lips. In a fit of spite, she dug her fingers into the tender spot at the back of his arm-pit. He growled his displeasure and smacked her thigh. Jiliana cried out, muffling the sound against his neck.

At long last he found her golden pearl, pinching it hard between his fingers until Jiliana thought she could take no more. Pleasure blossomed deep inside her, the storm strengthening to a major force, and still she needed...still she ached.

As if he knew her every thought, Graham picked her up and carried her to the bed. In the shadows she could feel him smile when she refused to uncurl her leg from his. "Have it your way," he said smugly, nibbling at her ear. "You are welcome to come standing up."

Graham finally did what she wanted, spreading her open to breach her jeweled gate. She gasped when his finger speared high inside her, rough and demanding. His thumb circled her golden pearl, working the nub with a frenzied glee.

But she wasn't ready to come for him so soon. Before he could guess her intent, Jiliana dropped to her knees before him, untying his breeches with hands that shook. She had to touch him, feel him firm between her fingers, taste him as she took him into her mouth.

Wrapping her arms around his hips, she slid his pants down, nuzzling her face against his stomach as the length of him broke free. He splayed his legs wider and tangled his fingers in her hair, guiding her mouth to his swollen flesh.

She had no thought of resisting. He could own her in the dark of the night when she was pliant and soft as the finest spun silk. She took his mass into her mouth, letting him thrust deep inside. His thighs trembled as she sucked him, his strength given over to the pleasure she offered.

And tonight she would offer him all of her. Anything he demanded...anything he craved. She would be his slave and rule him forever. He pulled out and drove into her once more, his flesh sliding between her lips to lodge at the back of her throat. In answer, she relaxed and tried to take him even deeper, hearing his grunt of pleasure as she swallowed more of his turgid length.

Jiliana knew he watched...she could feel his eyes tracking her every move. She lifted her chin so he could see better, admire the view of her kneeling at his feet, her only intent to serve his every need.

"More," he growled, when she blinked up at him through her lashes. His expression made her body pulse...raw, hungry, the conqueror claiming his reward.

Jiliana sucked him faster, one hand moving to slide between his legs, circling over his heavy sac. He groaned when she squeezed, his eyes closing in rapture at her touch.

"Enough!" He pulled on her hair, forcing her to stand. "The only way I will come tonight is with my jade scepter thrust to the root through your perfect gate of jewels."

She trembled at the look on his face. Possessive. Commanding. Leaving no room for indecision. He grabbed her hips and jerked them to his, his cock sliding between her thighs, hot and thick and ready to take her.

For an instant she stiffened, wanting to run away as she gazed into his eyes. As open as a cloudless sky, they devoured her slowly, dragging her into his heart one devastating inch at a time. He would make her give him everything...body, soul, the perfect and the tainted. Did he know how much he asked?

One corner of his mouth turned up, elegant and tender. "I promise you'll like it." The last of her resistance faded as he trailed kisses down her cheek. Graham never made a promise he didn't intend to keep. "Show me that other tattoo," he added in a whisper.

She giggled and bent her head, letting her hair fall over him like water as she bared the mark at the base of her neck.

She felt him trace it with his fingers, the swirling characters unreadable and strange. "What does it mean?"

Jiliana's cheeks grew hot. "My friend. I had it done for you... I never thought you would ever see it."

"I love you." He cupped her face in his hands and bent to kiss her, his mouth slanting over hers in growing urgency. When he speared his tongue between her lips, she whimpered her need, her hips bucking against his, the mass of his cock smoothing along her slit.

A hoarse moan escaped him as he dragged his mouth from hers. "Come here." Taking her hand, he led her to a chair draped in velvet. A small chest sat on the floor beside it and Graham threw open the lid, pulling out a long strand of pearls.

He draped the jewels around her neck, nodding in satisfaction when they dropped cool like the ocean they came from down her stomach. "Just as I'd imagined. Perfect." With a true glee, his fingers plucked a second strand of jewels from the chest...rubies, she thought as they gleamed rich and red.

226

These, also, Graham draped around her neck. "Exquisite."

When he pulled out a third strand, she shook her head. "What is all this?"

A chuckle rumbled deep in his chest. "Just an idea I got from the prince. Humor me, I'll have to give them up when he finds out they're missing."

"Graham—you didn't—?"

"Shhhhhh." The last necklace fell across her breasts, the emeralds adding their color to the display. "Rare," Graham finished, his eyes alight with passion. "They suit you, my Jili."

She looked at the finery in wonder. The gems did look beautiful against her skin, and she felt like a princess wrapped in their richness.

But the shine of the jewels paled in comparison to the light in Graham's eyes as he sat in the chair. "'Tis beyond time," he stated, taking her hand and raising it to his lips, drawing her down with him. "One leg on either side of mine," he instructed, settling back until his cock thrust high against his stomach.

Jiliana's heart pounded. "Here?" She'd never thought he would take her this way.

"In my castle, I am the king, and you are my loving and obedient servant. Trust me," he added when she opened her mouth to refute his claim.

She knelt on the chair above him, uncertain and exposed until he bent his head to suckle her breast. The fire raged instantly, shooting deep between her legs in a rush that left her breathless and raw. She cried out when he bit down, feeling her nipple swell and tighten to a peak. He sucked harder, longer, drawing the first scream from her throat as the pain of her hunger blossomed anew.

"Go on. Scream," he commanded, turning his attention to

her other breast. "I owe my brothers at least a month's worth of sleepless nights." He flicked his tongue across her skin in long wet strokes, never quite giving her the pressure she needed.

"More," she begged, arching her back, grabbing fistfuls of his hair. "Please," she said louder when he continued to tease. She could feel her body grow damp with need, the wet of her gathering between her legs.

Her scent rose thick and sweet between them. This time Graham was the one to groan as he tucked one hand between her thighs and spread her tender folds of flesh. She gasped when he breached her with his finger, sliding it steadily higher into her body. She whimpered when he pulled it out again, her nails digging into his shoulders.

In response, he added another finger, stretching her past his earlier explorations. She jerked, but did not flinch from the touch, needing even more to soothe the heady ache. He continued to lick and suck her breasts as his fingers plundered her gate of jewels, his thumb rubbing her golden pearl, rasping over the knot of flesh until she screamed his name for the world to hear.

"Ahhhhh...uhn..." Her breath caught in a wordless cry as the pleasure took her over. She was ready...slipping into the bliss...her hips moving desperately against his hand, when he suddenly stopped and slid his fingers free.

He clamped his fists around her hips as he positioned the tip of his cock against the very opening of her cunt. It lodged heavy and insistent between her outer folds of skin, a demanding force that would not be denied.

"Relax," he whispered when she resisted, her thighs tightening to hold him away. "What do you need me to do?" There was concern etched across his face...and love...and need.

She traced the scar upon his cheek. It made him look

dangerous and desirable. She shook her head and moved to kiss him, sighing when her mouth met his. "Nothing," she said against his lips, pulling his hands from her hips to place on the arms of the chair.

He grinned and curled his fingers into the velvet—they had played this game before—and waited with infinite patience while she braced her hands on his shoulders and lowered herself upon him.

A cry escaped her when the head of his cock met her tight and swollen sheath. She wanted to pull back and ask him to give her more time, but the clench of his jaw told her he couldn't be dissuaded. She sank down another inch, trying her best to accept him, and whimpered in distress when his cock stretched her even more.

"Jili." Graham's voice was thick as he lifted one hand and tucked it between her legs. "Let me help." His fingers clamped around the bud of her clit, smoothing over the knot of flesh until the need began to build anew.

As the wave of pleasure swirled over her, Jiliana's body relaxed, the slick walls of muscle parting to let him pass. She arched her back as the rhythm consumed her, rising and falling in time with the touch of his hand.

He grunted in satisfaction when her thighs met his, his cock settled inside her to its very hilt. To her utter amazement, he stood and carried her to the bed, the length of his flesh never once slipping free. "My turn," he whispered, laying her on her back, his hips flexing in a movement that thrust him even deeper.

Jiliana cried out as he moved to withdraw, clamping her thighs tight. He snarled and grabbed her knees, pushing them down to the bed.

"Give way," he told her, refusing to let her go. "I have better things to do than fight you all night long...but I will, if you insist."

Her legs began to tremble as she stubbornly resisted, until he lowered his head and kissed her, his tongue seeking entrance into the heat of her mouth. She opened to the assault, dragging her fingers through his hair in a frenzy of rising want.

"Ahhhhhhhhh......." She screamed when his cock thrust high into her again, the sound muffled by the pressure of his mouth on hers. Her body burned where he burrowed inside her, her cunt clenching around him in both pleasure and pain. One hand found the pearl of her clit while his other rested above her shoulder, keeping her locked in his embrace as he took her time and time again.

She shivered as the fire consumed her, the release rising strong and hard and fast. Graham looked at her and smiled when her hips arched against him. "Scream, little one," he told her, giving her clit a final pinch. "Scream loud enough the whole damned world can hear."

She did...a banshee wail that ripped apart the night when she fell over the edge and into the pleasure that only Graham could give. Her gate of jewels clamped around him, fisting his scepter in its slick embrace. He added his cries to hers, scraping them both across the bed as he drove into her a final time, his own body jerking in wild abandon as he shot his seed deep into her cunt.

And when she thought they had reached the end, Graham rolled her over onto her stomach and spread her legs once more, his tongue wiggling into the tiny crease of her ass. She squirmed against this new invasion, gasping as his tongue burst through the ring of muscle, her body already hungry for more.

"Graham...you cannot possibly mean to—"

"I absolutely can," he answered, stretching out across her back, one hand trailing down her stomach to strum her golden pearl. "Trust me," he mumbled against her neck. "I promise you'll like it."

Chapter Seventeen

Jiliana stood and faced the rising sun, her *katana* balanced in her hands, the metal throwing off sparkles like diamonds as the shifting light caressed it. It was the most beautiful thing she had ever owned...and it had almost cost her everything.

She would never be able to trust herself with it. It was too much a temptation...too much a need she could not control. With it, she would kill again...she knew it of a certainty. Without it, she would have a chance at a life of joy and love.

The forge was blazing when she arrived, the smith having started it early as instructed. The fire danced like a living thing...a lover's caress that would smolder and destroy.

"Thank you," she said, motioning the smith to leave. "I will call you when it is done." She glanced at the blade a final time before she plunged it into the fire and watched the metal burn into an angry red line. Then, when she thought it was hot enough, she pulled the sword out and dropped it in a trough of water, the steam hissing a cry as if begging her to stop.

After it had cooled...when the metal had lost its structure and grown brittle, Jiliana laid it over the anvil and hit it hard with a hammer. It shattered after the very first blow, falling to the ground like leaves after a storm.

She sighed. It was done, and no skill of man could piece it back together.

"What now?" Graham came to stand next to her, looking down at the broken weapon, his expression as relieved as hers was tense.

"Toss it out...throw it away. That part of my life is gone forever." She took Graham's hand and pressed it to her cheek. "'Tis a small price to pay for all I've gotten in return."

Graham wrapped his arm around her waist. "You don't need it. You can still whip any man in Westmyre...except for me, of course," he finished with a wink.

They were married late the next afternoon. Graham's brothers swore they were the worst looking couple they had ever seen, and Jiliana had to agree as she looked at the scar puckering Graham's face, the bandage wrapped around his wrist, and touched the bruise that still blossomed on her jaw.

Not that she cared a single bit. She loved him—his heart, his spirit, his honor. The strength of his arms when he held her in the night, the way he tugged her hair when he was in the mood for fun...and more. And she loved every single scar that marked his body, knowing he had earned them while fighting for her life. She would never have asked him for even half of that.

He ran his finger under the ruffled collar of his tunic, throwing his brothers nasty looks every time one of them guffawed or chuckled. "They made me wear this on purpose," he muttered in Jiliana's ear, "*the bastards*. Along with these sausage-casings they have the nerve to call breeches."

She laughed, running her gaze over the skintight leggings that looked to burst at any moment. "Those were the prince's idea."

He glared at her with enthusiasm. "And I have already returned the favor."

The blare of trumpets announced the arrival of the royal family. The king and queen stepped down from the carriage and were seated with the Dunmores. The prince rode in last, formally dressed in his best suit of armor, doing all he could to impress the crowd that had lingered to catch sight of the celebration and share in the feast that was to come.

Graham nudged Jiliana in the side as he turned to watch the prince approach, the sheer breadth of his smile a warning that something was up.

"Graham," she warned following his gaze. "What did you—"

Her words died off as the first piece of the prince's armor fell crashing to the ground. It was followed by another and another and another until the man sat fuming atop his destrier in only his gauntlets and quilted underwear.

"Duncemore," he bellowed as the crowd dissolved into laughter that not even the king and queen could hold back.

"Yes, brother," Graham answered calmly, making no move to go to his aid. "Is there a problem? Looks as if your lacings didn't hold. 'Tis a shame. Your squire should be fired."

An aged scribe stepped up to perform the service, the frown on his face in marked contrast to the glitter of joy that shone in his eyes. "Silence," he ordered, satisfaction softening his expression as everyone hastened to obey.

"Cousin Joseph," Graham greeted with a grin. "Get this damned thing over with so I can put on some real clothes before my balls fall off."

The old man snorted and shook a finger beneath Graham's nose. "You listen to me, you mannerless oaf. If you interrupt me again, I will perform the long ceremony...the one that has an hour of prayer built into the middle."

Jiliana grinned when she saw Graham's face pale. But he didn't say another word out of turn until his cousin pronounced them man and wife.

His hand trembled when he reached into his shirt and pulled out a beautiful pouch of silk. "For you," he said, his expression as pleased as she had ever seen it. "A wedding present. Go on, open it."

Her hand shook worse than his as she untied the ribbon and pulled the gift free. The necklace gleamed in her hands, reflecting the light in an elegant and familiar manner. She stared at it for a long time before she could say a single word. "How did you...why did you?"

"Do you like it?" Graham ducked his head and glanced at her through his lashes. "I thought we could pass it down to our daughter...when we have one...and she could pass it down to hers. A token of the woman who saved the life of a prince and was a warrior of unequalled courage and skill. Shite, Jili, say something. I didn't totally muck this up...did I?"

A tear glistened on the necklace, followed by more as Jiliana acknowledged the magnitude of his gift. Like the broken pieces of her katana, bound in silver and crafted into something beautiful and new, so had she been born again in the fire of Graham's love. He had given her back herself...and made her stronger in the process.

"It is perfect," she assured him, turning so he could clasp it around her neck. It rested solid and comfortable against her skin, a reminder of all that she had lost and all that she had gained. "I love you, *baka*," she managed between her tears, throwing her arms around his neck and crushing her body to his.

"Oh hell," he said in a strangled tone, refusing to release her, as his body jumped in expectation. "I think I just split these damn breeches in two."

Epilogue

"I have a surprise for you."

Snapdragon, Pansy and Rose frowned at Graham's pleased expression, their own faces shuttering in disbelief.

"He's being too nice, Rose," Pansy said, glaring up at him from the table. "He's never nice. It's a trap of some sort."

Jiliana stood next to him and smiled, calming their suspicions. "He means it, this time," she said with a laugh, holding out her hand. "Come on, Lila's waiting."

At the mention of the younger woman's name, the three fairies perked up. The girl had treated them like royalty ever since they saved her from the assassin's blade. They flew to Jiliana's shoulder, ignoring Graham completely. She took them out to the side of the castle where a newly walled garden sat atop a hill.

Lila waved excitedly, opened the garden-gate, and ushered them in. "Well...what do you think?" She pointed to a tiny cottage set amidst a bed of clover, the building trimmed in lattice work, and framed by a porch beneath a shady roof. "Don't you just love it?" She knelt on the ground and pushed open the door. "Come take a look."

Snapdragon was the first to float down, banging on a pillar as if to test its strength. "Nice work." She arched a brow at Graham. "You didn't do it."

He laughed, the rumble pleasant in the air. "Wynn made it, actually. But 'twas my idea to begin with."

Pansy and Rose joined Snapdragon on the porch and peered through a miniature pane of glass. The house was filled with furniture and strewn with perfectly matching carpets.

"It has three bedrooms," Jiliana stated, counting off her fingers. "A kitchen, formal dining room, pantry, and something Wynn calls a solarium." She pointed to a glass structure butting off the back of the house. "Did I miss anything?"

Graham thought it over and shook his head. "Nope...oh, wait," he amended, placing a box on the porch. "I think you forgot these."

Rose hesitated, her hand on the lid. "Is this for us?"

"Of course it's for us." Snapdragon elbowed her aside. "Who else could possibly fit inside?" But she peeked at the humans from beneath her lashes as she realized how special their little cottage was.

"We know how much you must miss your home." Jiliana sat on the blanket of clover, her voice gentle. "We hoped—" She stopped as her eyes filled with tears.

"We hoped you would come to think of this as your new home," Lila continued, giving her friend a hug. "At least until you grow strong enough to leave." She looked at each of the fairies in turn. "I don't know how I will ever repay you...but I promise to try."

Pansy sniffed, blinking hard as she pushed the door open and stepped inside. "Snapdragon, Rose, it's perfect. Come and see."

But Snapdragon had already stuck her head into the box, squealing in delight as she pulled out the pair of bugs. "Crickets!" They started to sing as soon as she put them on the floor, the merry sound tinkling through the windows.

"And not just any crickets," Jiliana added. "I had them brought all the way from Eastshyre. They sing more beautifully than all the others."

"Maybe we could add a couple of those little salamanders I've seen near the river," Snapdragon said as she hurried to join Pansy and Rose. "And a dragonfly or two next spring."

As they watched their guardians make themselves at home, Graham, Jiliana and Lila smiled in true delight. All was well....at least for now.

About the Author

Gia Dawn has been a massage therapist, bookstore owner, and bartender—obviously having problems deciding what she wanted to be when she grew up. But she has always loved romance, from the very first books she snuck into church to read as a girl, much to the chagrin of her pious grandmother. She is happily married to her college sweetheart, and has two wonderful mostly grown sons. She loves her cats—all black, of course—and anything mystical or magical. You can visit her website at www.giadawn.com.

Cross a lawyer with a tale-spinning thief and throw in three
meddling fairy godmothers. Result? Magical mayhem,
hidden evils and dangerous desire!

Princess of Thieves
© 2008 Gia Dawn
Demons of Dunmore, Book 3

Snapdragon, Pansy, and Rose have their hands full as
Allard Dunmore meets the woman of his dreams—or rather
nightmares—in the impish thief, Jo. When her father goes
missing, she enlists Allard's aid to find him. And she won't take
no for an answer.

Sparks fly and love sizzles when Jo kidnaps Allard and
attempts to force him to help her. Despite his best intentions,
Allard is drawn into the web of dark secrets and heretical
writings that revolve around the renegade Jo and her
mysterious missing father.

As ancient evils chase them, and even allies become
enemies, the couple must learn to rely on each other to find the
hidden truth. When Jo herself goes missing, Allard's worst fears
are realized. How can he face losing the lawless beauty he has
come to love? Is he finally willing to put his doubts aside and
believe in her at last?

Available now in ebook and print from Samhain Publishing.

Enjoy the following excerpt from Princess of Thieves...

Allard watched Jo stab at the meal, knowing she choked down each and every bite. He was torn between the urge to wrap her slender body in his arms and whisper words of comfort, and the overpowering need to shake some sense into her stubborn little head.

"I would have thought a master thief like yourself would have no trouble stealing enough to eat."

Her chin jutted up. "I manage well enough. But there are others who need."

Allard felt her indignation. So that was why she was so damned thin. She gave most all of her spoils away. "Is that how you justify your choice of careers? It makes it right if you serve the needy?" He was interested in her answer.

"I don't justify anything." She continued to pick at her plate.

"What about those you steal from? Do they not need? Deserve the rewards of their labor? You deprive them." His lawyer's mind was getting the best of him, trying to pick her words apart to discover the hidden truth of her.

"I trade when I can."

That got his attention. "And what do you trade, princess?" He didn't know if he really wanted to hear the answer. If she traded herself—

"You think I'm a whore." There was a condemning twist to her mouth.

"I admit the thought did cross my mind. Are you?" he demanded when she settled to silence again. He didn't know why he cared. He'd known many women who sold themselves for a living. He'd paid them handsomely and enjoyed their services on many a lonely night.

She gave a bitter laugh. "Do you want to trade, Dunmore? My body for your work?"

Those amazing lavender eyes held a challenge Allard could not resist. He bared his teeth, no pretense of humor in the gesture. The surge of need rose between them again, and he let it sink into his awareness, a tide of want that settled hard between his legs.

He could sense her nervous attraction. Her hand rose again to her throat. If she did sell herself, she hadn't done it often. In fact, he thought, as he watched the blood surge up her beautiful neck and into her cheeks, he was willing to bet she had never sold herself at all.

"Would you agree?" The question slipped from his lips to hang heavy in the air. He slid his finger down the valley of her breasts to rest at the edge of her bodice. A small movement to either side would have his hand cupped across one tip. The anticipation of palming one tightly pearled nipple kept Allard poised on the edge of the chair. "Say the word and the deal is done," he whispered in her ear, giving into the urge to nuzzle her creamy skin. It was soft from the bath and lightly scented of sandalwood.

Her eyes grew huge, the pupils swelling to almost eclipse the lavender rim. She ran her tongue across her lips and Allard froze in expectation. "You would not be cruel." The phrase came out more like a plea.

Allard's smile softened. "I am not a cruel man." When she gave a slight nod of agreement, he still hesitated. "Was that a yes?"

She nodded again, lowering her eyes. "Yes." He could feel her tremble when he lifted her chin once more.

"And now you will tell me the truth." He ran his thumb over her lower lip. "Have you traded yourself in the past?"

She swallowed when he moved his hand to cup her nape, allowing the other to inch slowly over one breast. The nipple was big and swollen beneath his palm. "N-no," she stammered as he pulled her head back, baring her neck even more.

He had not even noticed her hair was the color of spun honey, but now that it had almost dried, it spilled in a golden fall across his arm. Mmmm, he thought, her other curls would be golden, also. And if he knew his women, her breasts would end in proud pink tips. He liked pink and gold. He ached for pink and gold.

"That is a very good thing." He tried to pull down her bodice and cursed when the shawl hid her skin. It quickly landed in a pile on the floor.

A whimper floated from her lips as he bared the nipple to the light. It was pink.

Beautiful, dusky, rosy pink. He rolled it between his fingers and watched as she bit her lip against the pleasure. He plucked it once again before dipping his head to nibble at the pebbled flesh. She shook at his touch and he felt the moan that rumbled in her chest, but she did not let one sound escape her.

Allard lifted his head to see her eyes clamped tightly shut and her hand knotted into a fist at her throat. He knew she wanted, he could smell the sweet desire that drifted from her flesh, but she was unwilling to admit it, too afraid to let herself go.

With a sigh of regret, Allard tucked her so soft breast back into the gown. This was a deal he would not keep. Every muscle in his body screamed in protest as he untangled his fingers from Jo's hair and bent to pick up the flimsy shawl and wrap it around her shoulders again.

Jane Seville would be proud of him, he thought, wanting to kick her lovely ass. He had learned. Coercion almost amounted to force, especially since he knew how much Jo was willing to give for her cause.

Jo blinked one eye open in confusion. "Did I do something wrong?" Her words were half muffled, quiet and concerned.

Allard traced a finger down her cheek. "I will not trade my services for sex."

She grabbed his hand and placed it again on her breast. Her own fingers were as cold as ice. "I need you to take this case. Please, whatever you want."

"Princess—"

"Why on earth do you call me by that silly title?" A spark of defiance blazed in her eyes.

Much better, Allard thought. "Princess? You are my most fascinating princess of thieves." He chuckled when her mouth opened and instantly shut again.

She frowned and pressed his hand harder against her still turgid nipple. Allard wanted to scream in frustration. And then he wanted to mouth that tender flesh again, dragging his lips lower and lower until he could feel her golden curls wet against his cheek as he slipped his tongue into the heat and need of her. Then he wanted her to return the favor in full and greater measure.

"You will come to my bed, make no mistake about that," he assured her, allowing his thumb to rasp over her breast. Her breath caught in her throat and he knew he was making progress, so he let his other hand drop to rest at the top of her thigh. Her hips jerked to meet his touch. This time the cry escaped her. "So, you want as much as I do." His fingers slipped between her legs and he rubbed them slowly against her, feeling for the outline of her body beneath the heavy folds of cloth.

His own breath caught when she shifted her legs apart, ever so slightly pushing back against his hand. "My princess," he whispered as he finally let his lips take hers.

Peppermint candy. She still tasted of peppermint, clean and fresh. Allard drank deep of her, thrusting his tongue hard into her mouth as his hand slid faster against her sex. He fumbled at the material, searching eagerly for the knot of her clit, rumbling his satisfaction into her mouth when his fingers finally found the spot he sought.

An answering sound whispered from her throat, as her arms twined around his neck and she opened freely to his embrace. Her tongue answered the demand of his as he continued the kiss. His cock roared to brand new life, his balls tightening in expectation, warring with his conscience as they never had before. But it was a glorious war. He felt more alive than he had in months, aroused and intrigued and amazingly happy.

Then his mind turned to more important matters as he felt Jo's body begin to shake.

"Say my name," he demanded, pulling his mouth away. "And do not dare say Dunmore." His hand stilled. She buried her face in his neck.

"Allard," he urged again, giving her a bit of the touch she needed. "Say it."

"Ah—" she whispered, letting her teeth scrape his skin. "Allard." So soft he could barely hear it.

"Louder," he commanded, increasing the pressure on her clit again.

GREAT
cheap
fun

Discover eBooks!

THE FASTEST WAY TO GET THE HOTTEST NAMES

Get your favorite authors on your favorite reader, long before they're out in print! Ebooks from Samhain go wherever you go, and work with whatever you carry—Palm, PDF, Mobi, and more.

Samhain
publishing Ltd

WWW.SAMHAINPUBLISHING.COM

Printed in the United States
146241LV00001B/47/P